PEN PALS:
BOOK ELEVEN

ROOMMATE
TROUBLE

by Sharon Dennis Wyeth

A YEARLING BOOK

Published by
Dell Publishing
a division of
Bantam Doubleday Dell Publishing Group, Inc.
666 Fifth Avenue
New York, New York 10103

The trademark Yearling ® is registered in the U.S. Patent and Trademark Office.
ISBN: 0-440-40345-6

Published by arrangement with Parachute Press, Inc.
Printed in the United States of America
July 1990
10 9 8 7 6 5 4 3 2 1
OPM

For Gary, Brian, and Kevin

CHAPTER ONE

———◆———

Dear Rob,

Being cooped up in Alma Stephens School for Girls all winter does terrible things to the human brain. I'm turning into a major grouch, Amy is unbelievably grumpy, and even Shanon is acting kind of cranky. And if Palmer says one more word about her mother's mansion in sunny, fun-filled Palm Beach, we're all going to pack her up in a big crate and send her back there—air mail special delivery!

Don't worry, though. I've come up with a plan to get the four of us through the rest of February: we're going to redo our dormitory suite! We'll turn the sitting room into one huge sleeping area, and what used to be the bedrooms will become two mini sitting rooms. Now that I've worked out the details, all I have to do is convince my roommates it's time for a change. Wish me luck and write soon to let me know what you think of my idea.

Grouchily yours,
Lisa

Dear Lisa,

I say—go for it! Rearranging your furniture is a lot safer than punching out your suitemates. Or dyeing your hair green. But while you're changing things around, please don't toss out any major items—like your favorite pen pal, for example.

Keep me posted on "Operation Big Move." If it works out, the guys here at Ardsley might give it a try.

Your same old pen pal,
Rob

"I still think we're making a big mistake," Shanon Davis sighed, plopping down on the floor beside a stack of magazines and books. Glancing over at her roommate, Lisa McGreevy, she added, "It's going to take us the rest of the term to clean up this mess."

Shanon's prediction seemed right on target. Halfway through "Operation Big Move," Suite 3-D in Fox Hall looked as though it had been hit by a typhoon. Clothes were piled on every available surface, and most of the furniture was stacked precariously around the sitting room.

Palmer Durand came in to dump another armload of cashmere sweaters on her bentwood rocker, then frowned thoughtfully as she studied the scene. "With four beds in here, this room doesn't seem nearly as large as before," she pronounced. "We'll never be able to squeeze in our dressers."

Lisa shrugged her shoulders. "So? We'll leave them in the other rooms. This is supposed to be the sleeping area," she explained for what seemed to her the umpteenth time since the project began. "With things arranged this way, we're all going to have much more privacy. For instance, you can do

2

your nails or take a nap in one room while Shanon and I are in here listening to CDs. And at the same time, Amy can be in the other sitting room practicing her music."

At that cue, Amy Ho, the fourth suitemate, picked up her guitar and ran her fingers gently over the strings. "If you ask me, this move is right on time. It's totally cured my wintertime blahs," she piped up cheerfully. Her dark eyes shone as she began to hum "Cabin Fever," a song she and her pen pal John Adams had written together.

Shanon still wasn't convinced. Leaning over to rescue her favorite pink-and-gray striped sweatshirt from under a jumble of books, she folded it neatly on the bed. "I think I liked the old way better," she said tentatively.

"Don't worry," Palmer said. "Lisa's plans usually turn out just fine. Don't forget, it was her idea to put our ad for pen pals in the Ardsley *Lion*. Without our letters from the boys, this semester would've been totally boring!"

Shanon ran her fingers through her sandy hair, a slow smile chasing the doubt from her face. "I wouldn't go that far," she said, "but meeting Mars has certainly made this school year very special for me."

"Speaking of our pen pals, there won't be enough space beside my bed for the nightstand where I keep Sam's picture. I'll never be able to go to sleep without looking into his gorgeous gray, dreamy eyes," Palmer complained.

"No problem." Amy bounded up from her seat on the floor to drag a small Parsons table into the center of the new dorm-style bedroom. Retrieving the photos of their four pen pals, she placed them in a square on top of the table. "Now all we have to do is arrange our beds so they face our favorite guys," she said with a satisfied smile.

"Amy, you're positively brilliant!" Lisa exclaimed, grateful for her friend's support. To head off any further objections, she began tugging at the foot of one of the cots. "Come on, gang, let's do it! And as soon as we're finished here, we can go over to Booth Hall and check our mail boxes."

With the cherished snapshots safely in place, much of the tension drained from the room. The four girls worked quickly to stow away their belongings. In less than an hour, Shanon and Lisa's old bedroom had been turned into a cozy den furnished with the pink loveseat. And in the new sleeping area, three of the beds were in place and neatly made.

As the girls struggled to position the fourth cot, Lisa looked at the desk by the window and cheerfully announced, "I guess that thing will have to go. Otherwise, we won't be able to fit four beds in here."

"Oh, no!" Shanon protested, wiping a smudge of dirt from her flushed cheek. "If we take it out, we won't have anyplace to study."

"There's a small worktable in my old room," Amy offered quickly. "We can move that in here."

"Good idea," Lisa approved. "I've always hated that desk anyway. It's so ugly. I say we junk it."

Palmer nodded. "That's okay with me. I don't do all that much studying anyway."

"So we've noticed," Amy giggled, and Lisa gave Palmer a fond smile.

But Shanon continued to frown unhappily. "It isn't funny," she sighed. "The three of you can afford to goof off because your parents pay your bills. But if I don't keep my average up, I'll lose my scholarship," she said anxiously.

"Don't be such a worrywart," Palmer advised. "With

your brains you could give up studying altogether and still get straight A's! I wish I—"

Lisa cut off the protest with a wave of her hand. "She has a point, Palmer." And turning to Shanon, she proposed, "We can put your desk and all the bookcases in the other small room. That way we'll have our very own library. How does that sound?"

Shanon shook her head. "It won't work for me. The window in there faces the quadrangle. I'll never be able to concentrate with all that noise right outside."

"Hey, why are you being so uptight, Shanon?" Amy chimed in. "The rest of us are doing our best to make this work. Can't you just give the new arrangement a chance? Who knows—you may even wind up liking it."

And with that, all four girls started talking at once. No one noticed the knocking at the door until it became a frantic pounding.

"Oh, rats! It's probably Kate Majors," Lisa broke off their argument to say. It wasn't the first time the dorm monitor had to warn them about making too much noise.

"I'll get rid of her," Amy offered. Running her fingers through her mousse-spiked hairdo, she pasted a big grin on her face and headed for the door.

But instead of the bossy Kate Majors, she found Muffin Talbot standing outside in the hallway. Tears were streaming down her pale heart-shaped face.

"What's wrong?" Shanon asked urgently.

Muffin opened her mouth to speak, but all that came out was a burst of sobs.

"Are you hurt?" Amy queried, putting her arm around the weeping girl's shoulders.

Muffin shook her head "no"; then after a few seconds she nodded "yes."

"Which is it?" Palmer said impatiently.

Muffin finally managed a mournful wail. "P-please h-help meeeeeeee."

Amy gently drew the quivering girl inside the suite. "Okay," she said. "But we can't read your mind. You've got to tell us what the problem is."

Instead of answering, Muffin clung to Amy in a fresh fit of hysteria.

"We'd better quiet her down before Kate comes snooping by," Lisa said, closing the door behind them.

Shanon patted Muffin's arm soothingly. "Maybe one of us should go get Miss Grayson," she suggested in a low voice.

"No, we can handle it by ourselves," Lisa insisted.

The others nodded their agreement. They led Muffin into the big room, their dispute now forgotten. The Foxes of the Third Dimension, as the four girls who lived in Fox Hall's Suite 3-D called themselves, were once again a team.

CHAPTER TWO

When Muffin Talbot was seated on the bentwood rocker, her feet didn't reach the floor. Besides being the shortest student at Alma Stephens, she was also the most timid. It took a good ten minutes for Lisa to get her talking.

"It's about my room," she finally sniffled.

The other four exchanged puzzled glances.

"Did your lights go out?" Shanon queried.

At the same time, Amy asked, "Did you see a mouse in there?"

Muffin shook her head, dabbing at her eyes. "I thought I was so lucky when I drew a single at the beginning of the school year."

"But now you're afraid to stay by yourself!" Palmer jumped to the conclusion.

"I am not. In fact, I don't want to live with someone else," Muffin protested between hiccups. "But because Fox Hall's so crowded this term, they've put another girl in my room."

"Learning to share your space can be very hard," Shanon tried to console her. "It took the four of us a while before we got used to each other."

"You don't understand." Fresh tears welled up in Muffin's wide brown eyes. "Lorraine Murphy, my new roommate, is mean to me."

"Lorraine Murphy—isn't she the new student who transferred here from a school in Washington, D.C., last week?" Palmer asked.

"Uh-huh. She's in my biology class, and I overheard her telling Dawn Hubbard that she was fifteen," Amy offered.

"How can she be that old and still be a third-former?" Lisa wondered.

Palmer inspected her perfectly polished fingernails for chips. "The way I heard it, she's behind because she was out of school modeling for an agency in New York. She has the most fabulous clothes. Yesterday she was wearing a hand-knit Aran Isle sweater that I'd die for!"

"I understand her parents have tons of money," Amy added.

Shanon wrinkled her nose, not caring for the gossipy turn the conversation was taking. "Lorraine takes creative writing with me. We walked back to the dorm together the other day, and she seems like a nice enough person."

"Well, she isn't," Muffin declared. "Lorraine's always picking on me and calling me a munchkin." She blew her nose gustily before continuing: "She yelled at me just because I couldn't reach a magazine she wanted from the top of the bookshelf."

"She must be at least five feet, six inches tall. Why didn't she get it herself?" Lisa asked.

"She said she was too tired. Lorraine acts like I'm her servant. We've been living together a whole week, and she hasn't dusted or swept the floor once," Muffin complained, sniffing again.

"Have you asked her to do her share of the work?" Amy wanted to know.

Muffin dropped her gaze and shook her head. "I'm afraid she'll yell at me."

Shanon felt a tug of sympathy. She, too, was somewhat shy and easily intimidated. But at the same time, she couldn't believe that the problem was entirely Lorraine's fault. "Since you're so unhappy, maybe you should ask Miss Grayson to switch you to another room," she said gently.

Lisa waved away the suggestion. "This dorm's already overcrowded. The only way to handle the situation is for Muffin to get someone to switch roommates with her."

"Like who? All the girls I know are satisfied with their assignments," Amy said.

"There must be someone," Lisa insisted, but she couldn't think of anyone offhand. After a long moment of silence, she turned to Muffin. "You need a chance to pull yourself together, Muff. Why don't you hang out here with us for the rest of the afternoon," she invited casually. Muffin smiled for the first time.

Palmer was apparently bored with the whole subject. Standing up to stretch, she said, "Now that that's settled, let's go check the mail. We can finish cleaning up later."

With Muffin in tow, the four Foxes set off for Booth Hall. The postman had brought a bumper crop of letters, and the girls could hardly wait to share their treasure.

Back in Suite 3-D, they sat cross-legged on the floor, giggling excitedly as the first envelope was ripped open.

Dear Amy,
> *In the grand scheme of things,*
> *Mountains are merely gigantic piles of pebbles.*

9

Boulders tumble down the slopes
On an aimless trip to nowhere.
Rocks lay pressed into the earth
Eternally waiting for something to happen.
Dark and light are only an illusion.

I hope you like my latest poem. Sometimes I'm afraid that spring will never come again.

Yours truly,
John

When Amy finished reading the letter, Muffin's face creased with confusion. "That's really neat—I think. What does it mean?" she asked timidly.

"You have to read down the first letters of each line to get the real message," Amy explained with a smile. "It says, 'I'M BORED!' "

"So am I," Palmer muttered as she unfolded her letter. "Now let's get to the good stuff."

Dear Palmer,
This will be short because I'm really on a roll with a new song. It's called "Holding Hands," and I can't wait to get your reaction. As soon as I have the lyrics worked out, I'll send them to you.

Best always,
Sam

"Your pen pal is a songwriter?" Muffin asked, obviously impressed.

10

"One of the best," Palmer responded proudly. "He's the leader of a band called Sam and The Fantasy—and he really is fantastic!" She hugged the letter to her chest, her cheeks flushed with happiness. " 'Holding Hands,' " she sighed. "Aren't you wild about the title? I know Sam's writing this one just for me. He once told me that I've got the most gorgeous hands!"

"Wait till he sees your Passion Peach polish," Shanon teased, smiling brightly as she opened her own letter.

Dear Shanon,

Things are truly dull here at Ard-barf—bad food in the cafeteria, too many rules, and a bunch of guys no zoo would claim. But there are only two weeks left in February, so I guess I'll survive. How's your art class coming along? You do everything so well that I'm sure your project will be a masterpiece. Promise you'll still remember the little people when your work is hanging in the Met!

Boredly yours,
Mars

"I wish I could draw," Muffin sighed.

"So do I," Shanon mumbled, creasing the page into tight folds.

Lisa eyed her curiously. "What's the problem? I thought you'd ace art this term."

"I don't think I want to talk about it right now. Why don't you read your letter?" Shanon suggested.

Dear Lisa,

Not much to say except that I've been studying pretty

hard lately. Midterms are only a couple of weeks away and I want to stay head of the game. Got to run now.

Sincerely,
Rob

Lisa was more than a little disappointed. Her pen pal obviously hadn't spent much effort on the brief note. It seemed to her that their correspondence was getting shorter and less personal with each new letter. But her suitemates didn't seem to notice, and their visitor was obviously impressed.

"The four of you are the coolest, neatest kids in this whole school," Muffin raved. But then her face drooped with sadness as she added a soft, "I wish you were my roommates instead of that bossy witch Lorraine."

A sudden inspiration popped into Lisa's head. "Why not? You could at least sleep in here with us."

There was a moment of stunned silence before Palmer gasped, "Let's not get carried away, Lisa. We only have four beds, and I, for one, don't intend to share mine."

"I have a sleeping bag," Muffin said quickly. "I wouldn't mind bunking on the floor."

"That's perfect!" Lisa started to pace, planning as she walked. "You can leave your clothes and books in your own room. But at night, you can stay with us. That way, you cut your time with Lorraine to a bare minimum."

"That would be wonderful," Muffin breathed gratefully.

"We'd be packed in here like sardines," Amy objected. "Besides, Muffin's already unhappy with one roommate— how could she possibly deal with four?"

"I'd love it! None of you would ever scream at me or make me do anything I didn't want to do," Muffin replied. Her big

12

brown eyes filled, tears threatening to spill over again. "I promise I won't bug you. Please let me stay—I've never had any real friends before."

A vote on the subject produced two quick yeas from Lisa and Amy. Palmer was less enthusiastic, but after Muffin promised she wouldn't take up one hanger's worth of closet space, she went along with the others. When it was Shanon's turn to cast her vote, she hesitated. The suite's mixture of four distinct personalities sometimes caused conflict—what would happen if a fifth was thrown into the recipe, she wondered. But her roommates had already accused her of being uncooperative and she didn't want to prove them right. Besides, she really did feel sorry for Muffin. "I guess it'll be okay," Shanon sighed. Good sense made her add, "But before we do anything permanent, let's try it for a week and see how it goes."

CHAPTER THREE

———◆———

"What are you doing?"

The high-pitched voice made Shanon jump, causing her pencil to mark a jagged line through the drawing in front of her. She'd been concentrating so hard she hadn't even heard Muffin come into the suite. "Studying," she replied a trifle crossly.

Palmer and Amy were out jogging, and Lisa was visiting with Brenda Smith. It was the first time in days that Shanon had had a moment to herself, and she wasn't anxious to share it.

Muffin moved closer, frowning as she studied Shanon's sketch. "Why does your kitty have both eyes on the same side of its nose?"

"Because I'm practicing to be Picasso," Shanon tried to joke, embarrassed. In the first place, she wasn't drawing a cat—the art assignment was to sketch one of her room-mates. She snatched up an eraser and scrubbed vigorously at the paper, frowning her displeasure at Muffin. "I thought you had to go to the library."

"I finished early. Sorry if I disturbed you." Muffin backed away, her lower lip starting to tremble.

Shanon felt an instant burst of irritation, closely followed by a pang of remorse. Poor Muffin was so sensitive. Forcing her mouth into a smile, she ripped off the top sheet of the tablet and crumpled it into a ball. "It's okay," she said. "I wasn't getting very far with this anyway." She stood up to stretch, for the first time noticing the bundle of frothy pink material Muffin was carrying. "Is that a party dress?" she asked politely.

"No. My curtains." Muffin shook the folds from two sheer panels and laid them carefully on Shanon's bed. "Aren't they pretty?"

Shanon's hazel eyes widened in dismay. There were more than enough ruffles and satin bows on the curtains to make three bridesmaid's dresses. "They're very different," she commented tactfully.

"I've had them since I was a baby," Muffin said proudly. "Now that I'm staying here, I want to do my share of the redecorating. Besides, Lorraine hates them, so I had to take them out of my own room," she explained. "Will you help me hang them?"

Shanon's mouth flapped open and closed a couple of times before she managed to speak. "At the beginning of the term we all chipped in for the beige drapes because they match the walls," she finally said. "Everyone has to vote on whether or not we change them."

"I already asked Lisa, and she said nobody would care."

I care! Shanon wanted to say, but she swallowed the words before they escaped. It seemed that every time she opened her mouth she hurt Muffin's feelings.

15

"My mother made them herself," Muffin confided.

Shanon was caught in a difficult conflict. She thought the curtains were absolutely awful, but they clearly meant a lot to Muffin. "I suppose it'll be okay," she sighed, dragging a chair toward the window.

They had just snapped the drapery rods back into place when Amy and Palmer burst in from their run.

"Great workout," Amy panted, peeling off the black down jacket that matched her spandex jogging tights.

"My lungs will never be the same. It's so cold out there I . . ." Palmer's complaint trailed off as she stared open-mouthed at the window.

"These are Muffin's favorite curtains," Shanon said before her two suitemates could blurt out their reactions to the new window treatment.

"They're practically heirlooms," Muffin added.

"You don't say. Well aren't they special?" Amy said weakly.

"You took the words right out of my mouth," Palmer managed, swallowing hard. "But they're much too nice to be hanging in here. Suppose one of us spilled something on them?"

"No problem. They're polyester, and stains wash right out," Muffin assured her. "Thanks so much for letting me hang them here. I know it's silly, but they make me feel less homesick."

"Anything to make you comfortable," Palmer told her, an edge of sarcasm creeping into her voice.

"Oops! I forgot to bring the tie-backs. I'll run down to my room and get them," Muffin chirped. Her pale face was glowing as she dashed out of the suite.

No sooner had the door closed behind her than it opened again and Lisa breezed in. "Hi, everyone—what's up?" she greeted them.

"Muffin's curtains," Shanon said. "You really should have checked with us before you told her she could hang them in here."

"They're like something from the Sugar Plum Fairy's nightmare," Amy giggled.

Palmer raised a perfectly arched eyebrow as she glanced around the room. "They clash with everything."

The three joined together in the chorus, "Those things have got to go!"

Lisa took a quick look at the window, then gulped. "I had no idea they'd be so . . . pink. But we can't get rid of them now. Muffin will be crushed."

"That doesn't take much," Amy countered dryly.

"You said it!" Palmer agreed. "That girl can't take the least bit of teasing."

"I can't stand it," Shanon moaned. "She makes me feel so *mean!* I keep trying to be nice, but she keeps crying. It must be me!"

Lisa wandered over to the window to finger one of the pink ruffles. "I know Muffin's a little super-sensitive," she admitted. "But she's got a lot of good points, too. She's loyal, and kind-hearted, and she always keeps her promises."

"Well, she did help me with my math homework last night," Palmer said. "Maybe the curtains will grow on us."

"Like a fungus," Amy chimed in with a smile.

"Muffin would be okay if we could only build up her self-confidence," Lisa said.

17

"How are we going to do that?" Shanon asked skeptically.

"I've got a plan!" Lisa announced, lowering her voice. She pulled a slip of paper from the pocket of her magenta sweater and waved it triumphantly in the air. "I phoned my brother Reggie today, and he told me there's a guy at Ardsley who's interested in our pen pal project. He's an upperclassman, and Reggie says he looks like an actor. Not only that, next year he's going to be captain of the football team! He'll be absolutely perfect for Muffin."

"What would a super-hunk have in common with a girl who still sleeps with a night-light?" Palmer giggled. "He sounds more like my type of guy," she added slyly. "What's his name?"

Lisa dropped her gaze to the floor, a pink flush staining her cheeks. "Geordie Randolph," she mumbled.

"Randolph?" Amy's eyebrows peaked with surprise. "Is he any relation to Simmie Randolph?"

"His cousin," Lisa admitted sheepishly.

At the mention of the arrogant boy who'd once been her pen pal, Palmer gave Lisa an icy blue stare. "You've got to be kidding! Why would you want to stick a sweet girl like Muffin with a member of that creep's family?"

"Reggie knows Geordie really well. He says he's nothing like Simmie. Besides being good-looking and intelligent, he's a genuinely nice guy, and he's definitely sincere," Lisa reported. "Muffin's going to flip over him."

"Over who?" Muffin asked from the doorway.

"Geordie Randolph," Lisa announced with a big smile. Moving to the other girl's side, she handed her the slip of

18

paper. "If you're going to hang out with the Foxes, you've got to have a pen pal of your own."

Muffin's complexion went from pale to pink and back again as Lisa told her all about Geordie. At the end of the description, the small girl plopped down on her bed. Her face was a mixture of excitement and despair. "But I can't write letters to a boy," she wailed. "I wouldn't know what to say."

"You don't have a thing to worry about," Lisa said soothingly. "I'm an old hand at the pen pal game. If you get stuck, I'll be glad to help you out."

CHAPTER FOUR

Dear Mars,

I'm beginning to understand why van Gogh cut off his ear—art is a major bummer! In the first place, I have absolutely no talent. A blind gorilla with only two fingers could draw better than I can. And to make things worse, I seem to have a serious mental block about the subject. The minute I walk into the studio, I turn into a total klutz. Last week I bumped into Shirley Fisher's easel and wrecked the still life she was working on. And when I was mixing tempera, I added turpentine instead of water, so the landscape I painted looked like a picture of the Alaskan oil spill! Nobody wants to sit next to me in class anymore, and I can't say I blame them.

The bottom line is I may get my first C this term. I'm sorry for dumping my problem on you, but I need someone to share it with. My suitemates haven't been too helpful lately. If you can think of a way out of this, please write me. The sooner, the better!

Your desperate pen pal,
Shanon van Gogh

Dear Shanon,

You're a whiz at English lit., a brainiac when it comes to math, and you've forgotten more about history than most kids will ever learn. So, you're no Rembrandt—big deal! Nobody's perfect.

I think you have problems in the studio because you're trying too hard to be the world's greatest painter. My advice is to lighten up and have some fun with it. Just squeeze a few tubes of paint on a canvas and smear it around with your elbows. Everyone will think you've painted a dynamite abstract!

Meanwhile, don't let this get you down. Remember, I'm always in your corner.

Your number one fan,
Mars

"The movie playing at the Student Union tonight is something educational and totally boring," Amy announced between bites of roast lamb. "What Alma Stephens needs is a good social director."

Palmer helped herself to the mint jelly. "I'd vote for more interesting classes. There's an academy in upstate New York that has seminars on fashion coordination."

"What I can't stand are all the rules. There's no logical reason why we have to wear skirts to class," Lisa added to the list of gripes going around the dinner table.

"I guess nothing's ever perfect," Shanon spoke up wistfully. "Still, I'd rather be here than at any other school I can think of."

"I suppose you're right. Thanks to Mrs. Butter, at least the food is good," Lisa said, grinning sheepishly. "She really is a great cook. Hey, I thought you loved her lamb, Shanon."

21

"I do." But instead of enjoying the delicious entree, she poked it absently with her fork. The expression in her eyes was as bleak as a winter landscape.

"If you're not going to eat your dessert, the rest of us can split it. It's a crime to let gooseberry trifle go to waste," Palmer scolded.

Lisa turned to her roommate, her face reflecting concern. "You've been gloomy all afternoon, Shanon. What's wrong?"

"It's nothing." Shanon mustered up a weak smile. "I'm fine. Really I am."

"Was there another disaster in art?" Amy prompted.

"I didn't go to the studio today," Shanon admitted, staring down at her plate.

Palmer rolled her blue eyes to the ceiling, pretending astonishment. "I can't believe it! Shanon Davis, the most dependable, responsible student ever to walk the halls of Alma Stephens School for Girls, actually *cut* a class!"

"Leave her alone, Palmer," Lisa warned. And then in a gentler voice, she said, "You were okay before we went to math, Shanon. What happened?"

"This." Shanon fished a piece of paper from the pocket of her skirt and shoved it across the tabletop. Lisa carefully unfolded it and her eyes widened with surprise. It was the answer sheet from a math quiz with the grade marked in red across the top. "I got a B minus," Shanon said miserably.

"So? I made a C, and I'm thrilled to pieces," Palmer scoffed.

"But you didn't open a book. I really knocked myself out getting ready for that test," Shanon countered.

"Don't worry," Amy soothed. "Everyone has an off day

once in a while. Anyway, B minus is a fairly good grade."

"Not for me, it isn't. Until today, I had a straight A average in math." Worry furrowed Shanon's forehead as she continued, "I just can't seem to study in the suite anymore. It's awfully crowded now that Muffin's there all the time. Besides, she always wants to talk. It's extremely distracting."

"Why don't you just tell her you have work to do?" Amy suggested.

"Oh, I couldn't do that!" Shanon exclaimed. "She'd think I was being mean. There's only one solution," she said firmly. "Muffin has to go back to her own room. Our suite just isn't large enough for five people."

"Shh!" Lisa hissed, glancing at the nearby table where Muffin was sitting with Kate Majors and Brenda Smith. "She might overhear you."

Muffin caught Lisa's gaze, and smiling brightly she waved at the four Foxes.

"She really is a good kid," Amy observed, returning the wave. "She'd be crushed if she thought we didn't want her to stay with us anymore."

Now it was Shanon who looked wounded. "Which is more important, her feelings or my grades?"

"You're just in a little slump—your grades are sure to pick up soon," Lisa responded. "But right now Muffin really needs us."

"What about me?" Shanon wailed. "I need you, too!" An unaccustomed flash of anger turned her hazel eyes pure green as the other three girls exchanged glances. "Well, that's fine with me," Shanon said stiffly when no one said a word. "When I lose my scholarship you can move her into

23

3-D permanently and baby her to your heart's content!" And, snatching her coat from the back of her chair, she got to her feet and marched from the dining hall.

"We'd better go after her," Amy advised, pushing away from the table. "She's pretty upset."

The Foxes caught up with their suitemate halfway across the quadrangle.

Lisa grasped Shanon's shoulder and pulled her to a stop. "Don't be mad," she pleaded. "We can work this out."

"We'll just have to think of some way for you to have your study space without sending Muffin back to stay with awful Murphy," Amy offered.

Shanon scuffed at the snowy sidewalk with the toe of her boot. "You know, we've only heard Muffin's side of the story. It isn't fair to jump to conclusions about Lorraine."

Lisa pulled the collar of her coat up around her ears, shivering from a sudden gust of wind. "Muff says she's a rat, and I believe it," she said stubbornly.

"I think Lorraine's a liar." Palmer tugged a pair of leather gloves from the pocket of her fake-fur jacket and slipped them on. "I'm sure she made up all that stuff about being a model and acting in a Broadway musical when she was three. And she claims to have lived in at least ten different foreign countries."

"Her father is a career diplomat," Shanon said in her defense.

"And Murphy is a career thief," Amy charged. "Remember the dream Dawn Hubbard told us about last week—the one that was going to be the plot for the sci-fi short story she's writing?"

"Yes, but what's that got to do with Lorraine?" Shanon asked, puzzled.

Amy leaned closer to deliver the punch line. "Murphy stole Dawn's idea and used it in her own short story."

"I don't believe it. No one could be that dishonest," Shanon protested. "It's probably just a coincidence that their work is similar."

"Sure it is. Dozens of people write stories about green men from Zeerox who invade Earth and make copies of teenagers," Palmer scoffed.

"The way I heard it, Lorraine did change the name of the alien planet. Muffin said she spelled it X-E-R-O-X," Amy finished the tale.

"And if dear, little Muffin said it, it's got to be true," Shanon said sarcastically. "Did it ever occur to you that maybe Muffin is just jealous of Lorraine?"

"And maybe you're just jealous of Muffin!" Lisa shot back.

Tears welled up in Shanon's eyes as her suitemates all began arguing at once.

"Wait a minute," Lisa burst out. "I think I have an idea." Turning to Shanon, she said, "Muffin doesn't spend much time in her old room now. What if you went over there to study an hour or so each day. Then we could *all* stay in 3-D at night!"

"Maybe I will," Shanon said flatly. "At least I'd have a little peace and quiet." She started to stride away before her tears spilled over. But before she'd gone three steps, she turned back again to confront Lisa. "One more thing," she said. "You may think you're doing all this for Muffin's own good. But if you ask me, I think you just want her around so you'll have someone to impress with your opinions about everything," Shanon accused. "You're as bad as one of Dawn Hubbard's Zeerox aliens—you're trying to turn Muffin Talbot into a Lisa McGreevy clone!" And with that, she spun on her heel and raced away.

The other three girls were silent for a few seconds; then Amy and Palmer started to walk slowly toward the library.

"We've got some studying to do. Want to come along?" Amy called back over her shoulder to Lisa.

"No thanks," Lisa answered. "My hair needs shampooing."

As she stood motionless in the February twilight, Shanon's words echoed in Lisa's ears. There was more than a little truth to the accusation, she admitted to herself, cringing. She did enjoy Muffin's obvious admiration. But she also genuinely liked her shy, sensitive classmate and truly wanted to help her.

On the other hand, she and Shanon had been living together since the beginning of the term. More than just roommates, they had built a deep and caring relationship.

"It's not fair. I want to be friends with both of them—why should I have to choose?" she asked nobody in particular.

There was no good answer. Shivering as much from misery as from the cold, she shoved her hands in her pockets and headed back to Fox Hall.

CHAPTER FIVE

"Wait up, Shanon!" Lorraine Murphy's summons caught her just outside Mr. Griffith's classroom. Surprised, she turned to face the other girl.

"I just wanted to tell you how much I liked your composition. You're a terrific writer," Lorraine said enthusiastically.

"Thanks," Shanon replied, blushing with pleasure.

"I could tell from the paper you read that you're crazy about horses. Do you ride very often?"

She shook her head regretfully. "Only for a few weeks every summer when I visit my grandfather's farm."

"Riding is my passion. I have permission to go to the Brighton stables at least twice a week," the other girl confided as they walked slowly down the hallway. Her gray eyes were bright with pride as she added, "I have my own horse at home—an Arabian named Whirlwind. I've got an album full of pictures of him in my room. Would you like to see them?"

The invitation caught Shanon off guard. "I'd love to," she accepted shyly.

27

Lorraine did most of the talking on the way to the dorm, mostly appreciative comments about Shanon's work in Mr. Griffith's creative writing seminar. Remembering all the unpleasant things her suitemates had said, Shanon felt uncomfortable and guilty as she walked into Lorraine's room.

"I love the way you've decorated this." Shanon glanced appreciatively around: the drapes and matching spreads were in muted earth tones and a Navajo rug covered the floor between the beds. Wandering over to the bookcase, Shanon scanned the trophies that were on display. "Your folks must be very proud of you," she said, studying the engraving at the base of a loving cup.

Lorraine shrugged her shoulders, but instead of responding she picked up a thick scrapbook from the table in front of the window and handed it to Shanon.

The two girls sat cross-legged on the floor to thumb through the album. Lorraine's easy chatter and their shared enthusiasm for horses quickly broke through Shanon's normal reserve. In no time at all, they were laughing and talking as though they'd known each other forever.

As Lorraine got up to remove some sodas from a miniature refrigerator in the closet, Shanon watched her graceful movements with growing admiration. Lorraine seemed so nice that Shanon couldn't begin to imagine her bullying someone like Muffin Talbot.

Before she could stop it, a burning question popped out of Shanon's mouth. "I don't mean to be nosy, Lorraine, but what's really going on between you and Muffin?"

A shadow of sadness drifted over the other girl's face. She twisted a shining length of auburn hair around her finger and sat back down on the floor with a sigh. "I'm not quite sure," she began. "I guess we just got off on the wrong foot.

I was really hoping things would work out well between us. Roommates shouldn't argue—they should be best friends."

"Tell me about it," Shanon said. She and Lisa hadn't spoken to each other since their angry exchange in the quad two whole days ago. A wave of misery washed over Shanon as she thought of their once-close relationship.

"Right from the beginning, Muffin let me know she didn't want to share the room," Lorraine went on. "And she's so sensitive that I couldn't make the tiniest little joke without upsetting her. Once I said something about her height, and she went all to pieces. I didn't mean any harm, though—people are always teasing me about being tall."

"I'm sure the two of you can work it out," Shanon told her comfortingly.

"I hope so. But I wish she'd stop making up such—such ugly lies about me," Lorraine stammered. Lorraine's ivory cheeks were pale and there was a hint of moisture in her eyes. Talking about the dispute was obviously painful.

Shanon was instantly contrite. "I'm sorry," she murmured. "I shouldn't have brought it up."

"That's okay. It's a relief just to have someone listen to my side of the story." Lorraine closed the album and changed the subject. "My dad just sent me a new Tracy Chapman CD. Would you like to hear it?"

Shanon rose to her feet. "I'd love to, but I'd better take a rain check. I've got a ton of math to do."

"Me, too." Lorraine grimaced. "And I'm absolutely terrible with numbers. I didn't catch one thing Mrs. Terwilliger said in class today."

"You can borrow my notes," Shanon offered.

"It would be great if we could study together," Lorraine responded.

29

Before Shanon could object, the other girl began clearing a space on the table by the window. Dragging up two chairs, she waited expectantly.

Shanon felt uneasy. Considering the trouble she was having with her own work, she wasn't sure she should be tutoring someone else.

"I'd really appreciate your help," Lorraine urged. There was more than a little sadness in her gray eyes as she added, "I've been so lonely since I transferred to Alma Stephens. Most of the kids here are such snobs. You're the only one who's been friendly to me."

"That'll change once everyone gets to know you," Shanon assured her.

Lorraine nodded polite agreement, but it was clear that she wasn't convinced.

At a loss for anything else to say, Shanon took a seat and opened her math book. But halfway through the first problem, the lead in her pencil broke.

"Rats! I know there's another one in here—somewhere," she said, digging through her bookbag.

"Here's one." Lorraine slid a replacement across the table.

Shanon picked up the mechanical pencil, an obviously expensive one that had four different colors of lead tucked inside its transparent barrel. "I'm not sure how it works, and I wouldn't want to ruin it," she said dubiously.

Chuckling, Lorraine showed her how to use the writing instrument.

"This is so neat!" Shanon exclaimed. "Maybe I'll save up my allowance for the next three months and buy one just like it!"

"You can have that one," the other girl offered nonchalantly.

Shanon's eyes widened with surprise. "Thanks, but I really couldn't take it," she protested.

"Take it," Lorraine said. "My father's secretary orders those things by the gross. I'm glad to get rid of one." Then, to signal that the matter was settled, she went and got two more sodas and a bag of chips.

"I hate to be a nuisance," Lorraine told Shanon a few minutes later, "but could you start from the beginning and explain ratios to me?"

A few days later while all the other members of Suite 3-D were at the snack bar, Shanon took advantage of the privacy to write to her pen pal.

Dear Mars,

I'm really confused about the situation between Muffin Talbot and Lorraine Murphy. Lorraine is such an interesting and generous person. Yesterday, she gave me the most gorgeous butterfly clip to wear in my hair, and she's always willing to share the imported cookies her dad sends. Best of all, she's invited me to ride with her at Brighton Stables! She's sort of behind in some of her classes, though, so I'm helping her as much as I can. Unfortunately, I'm having a little trouble getting my own work done lately, but it's the least I can do after all she's done for me.

It's hard for me to believe that Muffin would deliberately lie about Lorraine. But on the other hand, it's even harder to picture Lorraine as the bad guy. I have a feeling that neither of them is totally at fault. Since they're both so nice, their disagreement is probably just some sort of misunderstanding. I'm going to do my best to help them patch things up.

Speaking of things that need patching up . . . the atmosphere in 3-D is still ten degrees below freezing. Lisa and I haven't settled our argument yet, and Amy, Palmer, and Muffin are all on her side. I feel like an intruder in my own room, so I haven't been spending a whole lot of time here.

Keep those letters coming, pen pal—I need all the support I can get.

Love,
Shanon

Mars's reply came in the return mail:

Dear Shanon,
Your new friend sounds super, but the old ones are also terrific. I don't believe that running away from your disagreement is going to solve it. Instead of avoiding Lisa, why not face her and offer to talk things through? The two of you have always been so close—I'm sure she'll meet you halfway.

I'm always here for you,
Mars

CHAPTER SIX

"I borrowed this outfit from Brenda Smith," Muffin confided, pirouetting in the center of the room so that Amy, Palmer, and Lisa could get the full effect. Brilliant orange harem pants sagged in floppy folds about her ankles. The red tie-dyed shirt completely engulfed her miniature frame.

"It's unique," was the most truthful comment Palmer could think of at the moment. She stared at Muffin's new hairdo, fighting off an almost overwhelming urge to giggle.

Most of the small girl's brown curls had been pulled into two stick-straight ponytails that stuck straight up from the top of her head. More than anything, she resembled a surprised Easter bunny. "I wanted my clothes to be cool like Lisa's, and my hair to be mod like Amy's. What do you think?" she asked.

"Well, you may have gone a bit overboard with the mousse," Amy said gently.

The sparkle in Muffin's wide-set brown eyes dimmed. "Tell the truth—you all hate the new me. I look ridiculous, don't I?"

"There was nothing wrong with the old you, Muff," Lisa

assured her. "You've got terrific skin and a cute nose. In fact, you're very attractive." And remembering Shanon's accusation, she added hastily, "But you need to find your own style, not copy someone else's."

"I want to fit in with the rest of you," Muffin sighed.

"You do. I'll help you work up a hairdo that sets off the shape of your face," Amy promised. She flopped cross-legged on her bed, her expression curious. "Has Geordie Randolph answered your first letter?"

Muffin dropped her gaze to the tips of her running shoes. "I haven't actually sent it yet."

"Why not?" Palmer demanded. "I thought you wanted to be his pen pal."

"I do, but I'm not sure that what I've written is right. Will you guys check the letter out before I send it?" Muffin pulled a crumpled paper from her pocket and passed it around.

Dear Geordie,

My name is Melissa Talbot, but everyone calls me Muffin. I've got brown eyes and hair. I like to do crossword puzzles and I have a pet Persian kitten at home named Puffin. Please write and tell me about your hobbies.

Sincerely,
Muffin Talbot

Palmer rolled her eyes in disbelief. "You've got to be kidding, Muff! This is a gorgeous upperclassman you're writing to, not your great-aunt Tillie!"

Amy peered over Muffin's shoulder, working hard to hide a smile. "And you might want to use plain dots over your I's," she suggested. "I don't think a jock would go for those little happy faces."

Lisa frowned at the sheet of lined notebook paper, rack-ing her brain for a tactful response. "It's not a bad start," she finally managed.

"It's no use. I'll never be radical and cool," Muffin wailed, her long lashes spiking with sudden moisture.

"Yes, you will"—Lisa grasped Muffin's arm and gave it an exasperated shake—"but you've got to stop putting yourself down. And you're not a wimp, so stop crying over every little thing that goes wrong!"

Muffin gulped back a sob and straightened her shoulders. "I'm not sure I can, but I'll try."

"That's good enough for me," Lisa said, grinning. "Now let's go over this letter and punch it up a bit." Her forehead wrinkled with concentration as she reached for a yellow pad. A few minutes later, she began scribbling madly.

Hi, Geordie!

This is Muffin Talbot, you new pen pal, coming to you live and in glorious color. My eyes are amber, but they darken to mahogany when I'm angry or sad. My friends say my hair is the shade of autumn oak leaves, but I think that's an exaggeration—it's actually an ordinary brown.

"Don't you think you're overdoing the rainbow bit?" Amy piped up.

"Poetic license," Lisa said blithely, going on to the next paragraph.

Word puzzles are my passion, and I'm crazy about animals. But more than anything else, I love football.

"I don't know the first thing about football," Muffin protested.

Lisa scratched out the last line, then nibbled thoughtfully on her pencil until she got an inspiration.

Football is really neat, and I'd like to learn more about the finer points of the game. When you write, it would be terrific if you sent me the name of a good book on the subject.

"Nice touch," Palmer approved. "Guys love to talk sports."

Muffin's face glowed with admiration. "You're so smart, Lisa!"

"Having a boy pen pal is easy, once you get the hang of it," Lisa said modestly as she went for the grand finale.

Also, please tell me all about your favorite hobbies, opinions, daydreams, etc. I'd like to get to know the real Geordie Randolph.

> *Looking forward to your first letter,*
> M.

The lone initial was signed with a curly flourish on the end. Muffin clasped the paper to her chest, barely able to contain her excitement. "I'm going over to the bookstore in the Student Union right now to buy some pretty stationery," she said, hurrying across the room. But she stopped with her hand on the doorknob and turned back. "Will you copy the letter over for me, Lisa? Your handwriting is so much more sophisticated than mine."

Flattered by the compliment, Lisa considered the request and nodded. "No problem."

As Muffin left the room, Amy shot her suitemate a dubious glance. "You're getting awfully involved with this project," she warned. "I hope you know what you're doing."

"I don't see any harm in helping a friend," Lisa replied defensively. "What could possibly go wrong?" Dismissing the subject with a shrug, she glanced at her watch. "I wonder what's keeping Shanon? If she doesn't come soon, I think we should go check the mail without her."

"She said she was going to stop by Lorraine's room. Maybe they got into a juicy conversation," Palmer speculated.

Lisa wrinkled her nose in distaste. "Shanon is spending a lot of time there lately. She hardly ever hangs out with us anymore."

"It was your idea for her to study with Lorraine," Amy said sharply. She strummed a few soft chords on her guitar, then laid the instrument aside with a gloomy sigh. "Suite 3-D isn't the same without her."

"Hi, guys," Shanon greeted them from the doorway.

"We were about to send a posse out to look for you," Lisa announced gaily.

"I picked up the mail. Amy and Palmer got lucky—you and I drew blanks." Shanon passed out the two letters, then set a tin filled with assorted bonbons on the table that held their pen pals' photos. "Help yourselves. They're really delicious."

"From France, no less!" Palmer crowed, selecting three of the candies. "Where'd you get them?"

"Lorraine's father sent her four boxes yesterday. She couldn't possibly eat them all, so she said I could share them with you."

"I think I'll pass. They're probably laced with a slow-acting poison," Lisa giggled.

37

Shanon frowned her displeasure. "If you'd bother to get to know Lorraine, you'd find out how nice she is. Unlike some people I know, she never, ever says anything mean about anyone."

"She doesn't have time. She's too busy stealing their ideas," Lisa countered.

"You're dead wrong about Lorraine," Shanon said sadly. "But I can see I'm not going to change your mind. Besides, I'm not here to start another argument—I came to apologize."

Shanon's announcement caught Lisa by surprise. She dropped her gaze, her cheeks coloring with embarrassment. "For what?" she mumbled.

"I was way out of line when I said those things about you and Muffin. She's lucky to have you on her side, because you're a terrific friend." Shanon drew in an unsteady breath and extended her hand. "Now can *we* be friends again?"

Words couldn't get past the lump in Lisa's throat. She clasped Shanon's hand, holding on tight. "Of course we're friends," she finally managed to croak. Clearing her throat, she added, "I'm sorry, too, Shanon. I should have been more considerate. I know how important your grades are to you. And I'll try not to knock Lorraine anymore."

"That goes for us, too," Palmer and Amy said together.

They all joined in a group bear hug, happy to have their four-way friendship renewed.

"Enough mush, gang," Palmer said, breaking the circle to wave her letter above her head. "We've got serious business to take care of."

CHAPTER SEVEN

———⬥———

Dear Palmer,
  *It would be a blast if I could have a successful career and
see my videos on MTV. But my greatest ambition is to write
music that really makes a difference. Speaking of which, I've
finally gotten my latest song in the groove. I got the idea
from a nationwide demonstration, the one where people all
across the country joined hands to show support for the
homeless. As I told you in my last letter, I call it:*

HOLDING HANDS
The day was gray and drizzly,
We made a living chain
Encircling those less lucky
We brought them in from the rain
Together we made sunlight
Together we fought despair
A shimmering, endless rainbow now hovers in the air
Young and old, all colors, let us now join hands
And create that living rainbow, the legacy of man

Chorus:
Hands to build,
Hands to heal,
Hands to banish hate.
Put your hand in mine, my friend—we'll keep this
*   country great.*

Write soon to tell me if you like it.

                                                                    Sam

"I think those are the most beautiful, touching lyrics I've ever heard," Shanon gushed.

Amy nodded in agreement. "When you answer Sam's letter, Palmer, ask him to send the music so I can play it."

"Your pen pal is really deep," Lisa said wistfully. Most of Rob's letters only skimmed the surface—chatter about his classes, movies, albums—and she wondered if he ever stopped to think about the really serious things in life.

"It'll never hit the charts," Palmer predicted with a frown. "People buy records for entertainment. All that hunger and pain stuff is depressing."

"You're missing the point, Palmer," Shanon objected. "The song is about togetherness."

"Yeah, but not the kind I thought it would be. I was expecting something more . . . romantic." Palmer tossed the letter aside, her dissatisfied expression blossoming into a full-fledged pout. Opening a bottle of iridescent pink polish, she began to touch up the tips of her nails, adding, "If he played that at a concert, the audience would be snoring before he got to the chorus. Sam O'Leary is—"

"Those lyrics are great," Lisa cut in. "And you know it.

You're only mad because the song isn't a moon, June, lovey-dovey thing starring Princess Palmer!"

"Romance sells records," Palmer huffed. "Let's just drop the subject and move on to John's letter."

"Great idea!" Amy piped up.

Dear Amy,

Maybe I should've started this letter, "Dear Abby," because I'm asking for your advice. A friend of mine knows this girl from his hometown who is interested in visiting him at Ardsley for a weekend. He can't decide what to do. What you think he should tell her?

Help!
John

Dear John,

If you want my advice, you'll have to give me a little more to go on. For starters: Does your friend like this girl? Is she a dweeb who he's ashamed to be seen with? What about their past relationship—were they ever serious? If so, did he dump her or was it the other way around? Write back soon and I'll tell you what I think.

Confidentially yours,
"Dear Amy"

"Does anyone have an extra stamp?" Amy asked after she'd dashed off the short note.

"Look in my stationery folder," Palmer directed sourly.

Opening the leather portfolio, Amy frowned. "There's only one in here. If I take it, you won't be able to mail your letter to Sam."

"I won't be needing postage tonight—or tomorrow, either," Palmer replied. She picked up her brush, vigorously stroking her hair into a cloud of gold around her face as she added a glum, "In fact, I'm not sure I'll be writing to Sam at all."

"You don't mean that! You're just disappointed about his song," Lisa protested, bouncing up from her bed. "A slice of pizza should put you in a better mood. Let's order a Monstro from Figaro's."

"That's a fabulous idea! And as soon as Muffin gets back, we'll throw on a couple of CDs and do some dancing," Amy added to the plan. "I can't remember the last time we had a pizza party in here."

"Count me out," Shanon said glumly. "I've still got two pages of math to do, I haven't even started tomorrow's history assignment, and the picture I'm working on for art is a complete disaster. Plus, I promised Lorraine I'd return some library books for her," she said, her shoulders slumping under the load.

Palmer raised an eyebrow. "If you're snowed under with your own work, why are you running errands for Murphy?"

"She has a migraine headache," Shanon reported. "She probably won't be able to make it to dinner this evening. I'm going to see if I can bring a tray to the room."

The other three suitemates exchanged uneasy glances.

"If she's that sick, maybe she should go to the infirmary," Amy suggested.

"She already has some medicine that her doctor prescribed. She says she'll be okay as long as she gets enough sleep," Shanon reported. Pulling a duffel bag from the closet, she began packing cosmetics and a change of clothes.

"Are you staying with Murphy again tonight?" Lisa asked, a note of irritation creeping into her voice.

"Lorraine and I are going to Brighton Stables at the crack of dawn," Shanon explained.

"My aunt is as limp as a dish rag for two days following one of her migraines," Palmer mused aloud, her eyes narrowing with suspicion. "If Murphy's in such bad shape that she can't walk across the quadrangle tonight, how's she going to ride a horse in the morning?"

It was a good question. To disguise the fact that she had no logical answer, Shanon changed the subject. "I wish all of you would stop calling her Murphy. Her name is Lorraine," she said.

There was an uneasy silence, which was interrupted by a loud knock at the door.

In reply to Palmer's "Who is it?" Kate Majors strode briskly into the suite.

"I came to see if any of you has an extra . . ." The older girl's request trailed off into silence. She readjusted her glasses on the bridge of her nose, peering around the suite with concern. "Why are your beds in the sitting room? And what's that sleeping bag doing in the middle of the floor?"

"Muffin Talbot is staying with us," Palmer explained.

Kate stiffened. "Who gave her permission to do that?"

"We did," Lisa answered for the group.

Kate shook her head in dismay. "It's against the rules for five girls to live in a four-bed suite. You should know that."

Amy fielded the hot potato. "Of course. But this is only temporary, Kate," she began.

But Kate didn't give her a chance to go further. "You're right about that. Miss Pryn would be very upset if she found out. You're going to have to put the suite back the way it was before."

And before any of the girls could argue, she marched out the door.

Lisa glared after her, fuming, "That Kate is so bossy!"

"She's only doing her job," Amy defended. "After all, she *is* the dorm monitor. And she's right anyway—we really should have checked with her or Miss Grayson before we made the move."

"So, what are we going to do now? We can't just throw Muffin back to the shark," Lisa protested.

"Lorraine isn't a shark," Shanon said stiffly.

Sensing another argument brewing, Amy stepped in. "I'm sure if we got to know Mur—I mean Lorraine—we'd like her a lot. As soon as she gets rid of her headache, why don't you invite her to hang out here in 3-D sometime."

Shanon flashed her suitemate a grateful grin. "That's a wonderful idea! Who knows? Maybe the four of us can even clear up the misunderstanding between Lorraine and Muffin."

"Misunderstanding, my foot!" Lisa snorted. "From what I've heard, I'd say that Murphy is a real terror. I don't see any point in giving her another chance to dump on poor Muffin."

"Well, the way I got the story, Muffin isn't exactly an innocent victim. Lorraine told me—" Shanon stopped abruptly, the subtle changes in her suitemates' positions making it clear whose side they were on.

"If you're so set on Muffin staying here, I'll just move in with Lorraine," Shanon said coolly. "As it is, I'm there most of the time anyway."

"No way! The Foxes can't split up," Amy responded, her face troubled.

"Of course not," Palmer agreed. "It wouldn't be the same here without you, Shanon," she added. "You *can't* move out! I won't even—"

"Wait a minute!" Lisa cut in. "Let's not get hysterical about this. It's not as if Shanon would be moving off the planet. She'd still hang out with us and share the letters we get from the guys."

Shanon could hardly believe what she was hearing. Her former roommate actually seemed eager to be getting rid of her. "If I have the time," Shanon said, giving Lisa a long, searching look. "Lorraine and I will probably be planning a lot of things we can do together." And flashing a brittle smile to cover her true feelings, she picked up her duffel bag and strode across the room. Shanon Davis was not about to stay where she wasn't wanted!

CHAPTER EIGHT

———◆———

Happy JIATING JIE, John!

In case you're wondering, Jiating Jiè (that's Chinese for "Family Holiday") isn't an official holiday. When I was little, my dad made it up for me because February was so dark, cold, and depressing. It's actually an un-birthday party for everyone in the family. We set off strings of firecrackers and exchange presents wrapped in red paper— that's the color of joy and luck.

Afterward, we eat apple pie and dim sum pastries. I'm luckier than most kids—because of my background, I get to pig out on two sets of luscious food.

For me, Jiating Jiè is the Fourth of July and Valentine's Day all rolled into one. This is the first year I haven't been at home for the celebration. I felt really bad about missing it until my folks sent a "Care" package full of gifts and goodies. I'm saving a fortune cookie to give you the next time we get together.

Best wishes,
Amy

P.S. I'm still waiting to hear more about your friend's problem with the girl who wants to visit him.

Dear Amy,

Thanks for sharing your super holiday with me—you really are a terrific pen pal!

My friend—we'd better call him X because he doesn't want you to know his real name—was once really hooked on Tricia. She's pretty, smart, and very popular.

Before X came to Ardsley, Tricia never paid any attention to him. But recently, she's been writing him some pretty interesting letters. She says she likes him a lot and that he's really a hunk.

X is totally confused. He doesn't know whether he wants Tricia to come visit him or not. He'd be very grateful for any advice you could give him.

Yours truly,
John

"It's perfectly clear to me what's happening," Palmer said, scooping a spoonful of ice cream from the banana split in front of her. She daintily licked off a dribble of chocolate fudge before continuing. "Ten to one, Tricia's not really interested in X. She just wants to get her hooks into some boy who goes to Ardsley."

"And she's using poor X just to get an invitation for a weekend visit," Lisa concluded.

"Or else she wants to make the other guy jealous," Palmer theorized. "Once she gets on campus, though, she'll drop X cold."

"That sounds like something you'd do, Palmer," Amy said dryly.

Palmer grinned. "Don't knock it—it works."

Lisa chose a French fry from the pile beside her burger and munched it thoughtfully. "John certainly knows a lot about this Tricia person."

Amy moved restlessly against the red leather of the snack-bar booth. "X probably gave him a complete rundown," she said, ready to dismiss the subject. "I wonder if Shanon got a letter from Mars today?"

At the mention of Shanon's name, Palmer's face turned glum. "We might never know. She hasn't spent much time with us lately," she said, absently stirring the remains of her ice cream into a gooey mess.

"I'm sure she'll come to 3-D tonight and share it with us," Lisa declared with more confidence than she felt.

The sudden attack of doldrums was apparently contagious. The three girls avoided each other's gazes, a thick gloom settling over the table.

"Sorry I'm late. I was helping Miss Grayson in the French lab," a breathless Muffin bounced up to break the silence. She slipped into the booth beside Lisa, her expression a mixture of eagerness and disappointment. "I see you've already started reading the letters. Did I miss anything good?"

Amy pushed the note from John across the table. "We were just trying to decide how I should answer this," she said.

Muffin quickly scanned the paper, then handed it back. "X probably shouldn't see Tricia. If she doesn't really like him, he could get hurt."

"Sooner or later, everybody gets hurt, Muffin," Lisa pointed out. "If X spends his life running from pain, the only way he'll go is backward."

48

"I think you're right, Lisa," Amy agreed. "I'm going to tell John that I think X should take a chance and invite Tricia to Ardsley. It could be very interesting for him."

"Now that we've settled X's love life, let's move on to mine!" Palmer said, pulling a square white envelope from her purse.

Dear Palmer,

Something's gone haywire at the Brighton post office. I haven't heard from you in ages. Just in case you're also having problems with your mail and didn't receive my last letter, I'm sending you another copy of the lyrics to my new song, "Holding Hands."

I'm entering it in a contest sponsored by the Chamber of Commerce. If I win (fat chance!), Sam and The Fantasy will get to perform it on "Brighton Byline," the local TV talk show. Wouldn't it be great if a talent scout from Hollywood was in the studio? How's that for a fantasy!?

Yours,
Sam

P.S. If you think the song stinks, you don't have to try to find a polite way of saying so. I can do without rave reviews, but I do need my friends' honest opinions. Please write soon.

After she'd finished reading, Palmer tossed the letter into a wastebasket. "So much for Sam O'Leary," she pouted.

Muffin peered at her incredulously. "Aren't you going to answer it?"

"Sure," said Palmer. "Someday. When I have nothing better to do."

"Are you serious?" Amy scolded her. "I can't believe you're so ticked off just because Sam's song isn't about you.

Helping the hungry and homeless is a much more meaningful theme."

"Save your breath, Amy," Lisa advised disgustedly. "On the day social consciences were handed out, Palmer Durand was at the beauty parlor—having her nails done!"

"Oh, all right," Palmer huffed. "If it'll make you three happy, I'll answer the dumb letter." She snatched up her notebook and, ripping out a sheet of paper, dashed off a reply. "How's this?"

Dear Sam,
   Your song is very nice. I hope you win the contest.
                                    Sincerely,
                                    Palmer Durand

"That'll certainly make him feel good," Lisa snickered.

"It's better than nothing," was Amy's good-natured appraisal. "It's your turn, Lisa. Let's see what Rob has on his mind."

Dear Lisa,
   Just a line to let you know I'm thinking of you. Classes are a drag, and Ardsley's food is still swine swill.

                                    All my best,
                                    Rob
P.S. My CD player is on the blink again.

Coming after John's juicy letter about X and Sam's big news about the songwriting contest, Rob's run-of-the-mill note didn't spark much enthusiasm around the table.

As Lisa angrily wadded the letter into a ball, Palmer quipped, "Don't throw that out. Save it for the next time you have insomnia—it's better than a sleeping pill." She faked an elaborate yawn.

"It was sweet of him to write that he was thinking of Lisa," Amy said loyally. Then she turned to Muffin, her face curious. "Have you heard from Geordie Randolph yet?"

A pretty flush stained Muffin's cheeks as she removed an envelope from her skirt pocket and laid it on the table.

"I'm dying to hear what Geordie has to say. Hurry up and open it," Lisa urged as Muffin carefully teased the flap of the envelope free.

Dear Muffin,

I'm not very good at describing myself, so I've enclosed a snapshot. As you can see, I'm just an ordinary guy.

Muffin stopped reading to peer at the photo that was paper-clipped to the top of the page. Her eyes widened and her mouth formed an incredulous O. Unable to comment, she passed the picture around the table.

"Wow! Look at that dimple in his chin," Amy breathed.

Lisa stared down at Geordie's deep-set blue eyes and the strong line of his jaw. "His smile is straight out of a toothpaste commercial," she gulped.

Even Palmer had to admit she was impressed. "But his cousin Simmie is just as good-looking—and also the world's biggest creep," she warned. "He—"

"There's more," Muffin interrupted timidly. "Don't you want to hear the rest?"

"Sure!" the other girls chorused.

As for hobbies, we have one in common. I'm crazy about word games, particularly super-tough crossword puzzles. I also love water sports. I spent last summer in San Diego, surfing and helping my uncle build a sailboat.

But enough about me—you're a much more interesting subject. While I was reading your letter, I developed a mental picture of you. Check it out, then write and let me know how close I came to the real Muffin Talbot.

Your handwriting is very bold. That tells me that you're probably athletic, independent, and maybe just a bit stubborn. I see you as being tall—probably 5'5" or more—and slender. My guess is that you're a take-charge person, a true leader. How am I doing so far?

You've got real style and I like your sense of humor. I hope to hear from you again very soon.

> *Regards,*
> *Geordie Randolph*

P.S. If you're really interested in football, there's a very good tape called "Countdown to Kickoff" that will give you the basics. You can pick up a copy at the video store in Brighton.

"What a great letter!" Lisa raved. Then, noticing Muffin's gloomy expression, she said, "What's the matter, Muff? It sounds like he's really interested in you."

"No it doesn't," Muffin said sadly. "Geordie Randolph just described you, Lisa, not me."

"Why wouldn't he?" Palmer said. "After all, it was Lisa's letter he was analyzing."

"When you answer him, maybe you'd better explain the situation," Amy advised.

Muffin's eyes misted with despair. "He's going to think I'm a total dweeb. Maybe I shouldn't even write back. It's obvious I don't have anything to say that would interest a guy like Geordie."

"Quit knocking yourself, you're a very nice person," Lisa said. "And don't worry—I can coach you through the next couple of letters."

Palmer stole a glance at the snapshot she was still holding. Geordie was even better-looking than his cousin, she decided. And his letter hadn't revealed any of Simmie's self-centered arrogance, either. An instant image of a sun-glazed California beach popped into her mind: Geordie, bronzed and muscular, was surfing on the curling crest of a wave. And in the fantasy, the lovely, bikini-clad girl waiting for him on shore was definitely not Muffin Talbot!

CHAPTER NINE

———◆———

The clock on the wall above the classroom door made an ominous, whirring sound before the big hand lurched toward the next position. Distracted from the problem on the blackboard in front of her, Shanon inched her gaze upward to check the time again. There were still five more minutes to go before fourth period was over. Would she be able to keep her eyes open that long, she wondered groggily.

Shanon had stayed up late the night before, listening to a batch of CDs Lorraine had just received from home. In addition, helping with her new roommate's social studies assignment had taken much longer than expected.

"You've been standing there long enough to grow roots, Miss Davis," the math teacher's voice came from behind. "If you're unable to complete the problem, you can always ask for assistance."

That brought a smothered burst of giggles from the back of the room.

"I'm almost through, Mrs. Terwilliger," Shanon mumbled, a flood of embarrassment heating her neck. Her palms turned sweaty as the chalk marks on the board suddenly failed to make the slightest bit of sense. But she started to scribble anyway. Even a wrong answer would be better than no answer. And anything would be better than standing there one second longer.

Luckily, the bell sounding the end of the hour rang before she could make a complete fool of herself.

"You may give us the correct solution at the beginning of our next class," Mrs. Terwilliger said sternly. "I assume you'll have the solution by then."

"Yes, ma'am," Shanon mumbled. Drawing in a deep breath of relief, she hurried back to her desk.

Lisa quickly rose from the neighboring seat. "You look awful," she said. "Do you feel okay?"

"I'm just tired," Shanon answered briefly. Avoiding Lisa's worried gaze, she gathered her books and prepared to leave.

"One moment, Miss Davis. I'd like to have a word with you," Mrs. Terwilliger called as Shanon slipped on her lavender down jacket.

"Uh-oh! That sounds like trouble," Lisa predicted under her breath. "I'll wait for you in the hall."

"Thanks, but I wouldn't want to hold you up," Shanon said coolly, still nursing a grudge from their last disagreement.

Lisa shrugged. "Suit yourself. You know where to find me if you need me," she said, hurrying away.

Shanon hadn't missed the hurt in her former roommate's eyes. She felt a twinge of guilt, but she pushed it to the back of her mind. A more immediate problem was waiting for her at the front of the room.

"Miss Davis, it's perfectly clear you came to my class unprepared, and that fact disturbs me no end," Mrs. Terwilliger began after all the other students had filed from the room. The teacher's expression was as stony as the faces carved on Mount Rushmore.

It was all Shanon could do to squeeze a shaky, "I'm sorry," past the huge lump that suddenly blocked her throat. She fixed her gaze on the tips of her shoes, wishing the floor would open and gobble her up. But since that escape route seemed highly unlikely, she swallowed hard and waited for Mrs. Terwilliger's next zap.

It never came. In fact, the woman's tone softened as she continued, "You're one of my brightest pupils, Shanon. But in the past few weeks your average has dropped a full grade point. Is something troubling you?"

The teacher's concern was almost as hard to deal with as her anger. "Things have been rather hectic lately, and I haven't been able to concentrate," Shanon admitted, fighting back the tears that threatened to fall. "I'll try to do better from now on."

"That's all I wanted to hear." The teacher gave her a gentle smile and, nodding dismissal, turned to a stack of papers on her desk.

As soon as Shanon left Cabot Hall, the slap of cold wind against her cheeks cleared some of the cobwebs from her brain. If she skipped lunch, she could put in some quality study time before French, she decided. Urged on by a determination to recapture her A in math, she ran all the way to Fox Hall.

But when she opened the door to the room she now shared with Lorraine, she felt like running right out again. The place looked as though it had been hit by a cyclone.

"What on earth happened?" she groaned.

"My closet was a mess, so I thought I'd straighten it out," Lorraine said, not taking her eyes off her reflection in the mirror over the dresser.

The black leather jodhpurs and short riding jacket she was wearing showed off her slender figure to perfection. She smoothed her red hair into a chic twist and, after pinning on a jaunty cap, turned around slowly for Shanon's approval. "What do you think of the outfit, roomie?"

"It's beautiful," Shanon responded absently. "Did you finish the assignment for Miss Grayson's class this afternoon?"

"Translating a paragraph of boring French is dead last on my list of things to do today," Lorraine replied. Gliding gracefully to her nightstand, she picked up a small white box and presented it to Shanon. She waited till Shanon had pulled out the mod watch with interchangeable bands and then said, "It's just a little something to thank you for drilling me on your social studies notes. I couldn't have gotten through the exam without you."

"The watch is beautiful and I appreciate the thought, but you've already given me too many things," Shanon protested, handing back the box. "I'm glad I was able to help you. Please don't feel you have to pay me for it," she finished firmly.

Lorraine's gray eyes misted with obvious hurt. "I didn't mean to offend you," she said. "But you're the first real friend I've ever had, and I just wanted to show you how much I like you."

"Just saying so is enough for me," Shanon said, touched by the sentiment. Though she'd wanted to catch up on her math, Lorraine's predicament suddenly seemed more pressing than her own. "The page Miss Grayson assigned you isn't very difficult. If we both work on it, we should be able to finish before class."

"It's really sweet of you to offer, but I'm cutting French today," Lorraine announced breezily. Her face glowed as she added, "I'm going to Brighton Stables instead. Douglas Pennington's promised to train me on the new cross-country course. And afterward, he might even ask me to go out with him."

Shanon's mouth dropped open. Brighton's jumping instructor was tall, dark, and totally gorgeous. He was also at least eighteen! "Third-formers at Alma aren't allowed to date," she said. "You could get expelled if Miss Pryn found out."

"But she won't find out, will she?" Lorraine glanced over at Shanon, her eyes narrowing. "You wouldn't rat on me, would you?"

"Of course not," Shanon protested indignantly. "But someone is sure to get suspicious if you don't show up for class."

"Not if you tell Miss Grayson I went to the infirmary with a bad migraine."

"But that's a lie!"

"A teensy-weensy fib," Lorraine corrected. She turned to face Shanon, her expression pleading. "Come on, Shanon—be a friend. I think I may be falling in love with Doug, and I've simply got to see him today. If you just do this one little thing for me, I promise I'll never ask you for another favor."

The appeal was hard to refuse. In fact, it was impossible. "Well, just this once," Shanon said uneasily. "But you'd better skip the date. I can't be responsible for covering that up."

"I'll be back by dinnertime for sure," Lorraine promised. Then she gave Shanon a brilliant smile and headed out the door.

Alone in the messy room, Shanon felt the weight of the world settle onto her shoulders. But the sad state of the room was only part of it. Although Shanon had seen Douglas Pennington flirt a bit with the tall redhead, she was sure he wasn't seriously interested. In her opinion, Lorraine was headed for heartbreak.

Even more troubling to Shanon was the phony excuse she had promised to give Miss Grayson. Why on earth had she allowed herself to be talked into lying, she wondered, too late. None of the Foxes—not even Palmer—would have tried to rope her into such a shady deal.

All at once Shanon was more lonely than she'd ever been in her life. Both her loyalty to Lorraine and her own stubborn pride wouldn't permit her to run to 3-D with her story. Fortunately, there was still one person with whom she could share the burden.

Dear Mars,

Why does growing up have to be so hard? Lately, it seems as if my life is full of corners—and I'm constantly getting shoved into one of them.

Part of the problem is that I miss my family. If I were home now, my sister Doreen would probably be telling me about her latest date. We do argue occasionally—mostly about her hogging the bathroom—but we're very close.

And since this is Thursday, Mom will be going to her ceramics class. We all teased her about the lopsided vase she made last summer. She just laughed and said she would only use it for crooked flowers.

Dad will cook dinner tonight. He's a terrific chef. The only trouble is, he uses every pot, pan, and dish in the kitchen. Doreen and I always ended up sharing K.P. duty with him, but I didn't really mind. After we finished the dishes, he always treated us to milkshakes.

I could go on and on, but I guess I'd better sign off now. Besides not wanting to bore you, I've got a ton of work to do. Thanks for being there for me—just writing about my family makes me feel closer to them.

Love,
Shanon

P.S. I'm still having a lot of trouble with math, but I think I can talk Mrs. Terwilliger into letting me take a makeup exam. Wish me luck.

CHAPTER TEN

———◆———

"Kate Majors saw Shanon in the hall just before lunch, so she's got to be in there," Lisa said, knocking harder on Lorraine Murphy's door.

"She's probably just taking a nap," Muffin supplied.

Lisa nodded agreement. Shanon had looked pretty ragged around the edges after math. "Well, we've got to wake her up. Where's your key, Muff?"

"Lorraine made me give it to her when I moved out. She said she didn't want me sneaking back to rummage through her stuff." Muffin shifted nervously. "Maybe we should find Kate—she can borrow a pass key from the office."

Lisa shook her head. "Don't you think that's a little drastic?" she said, rapping even harder. "Besides, Shanon's in enough hot water as it is."

After what seemed an eternity, a muffled, "Just a minute," came from the room.

The door opened and red-eyed Shanon peered out into the hallway. "What's up?" she mumbled groggily.

"Big trouble!" Muffin blurted out. "When we got out of Miss Grayson's class, we—"

"I slept through French? Thank goodness! Now I won't have to—" Shanon cut herself off in mid-sentence. There was no point in getting the other girls involved.

Lisa's eyes narrowed suspiciously. "You rack up three demerits for cutting class, and then you say 'Thank goodness!' All the studying you've been doing lately must be rotting your brain."

"I must have dozed off after I finished my letter to Mars," Shanon explained. "Was Miss Grayson very upset because I was absent?"

"We can talk about that later," Muffin cut in. "First, we've got to tell you about the accident."

Shanon shook her head to clear away the last remnants of her nap. "What accident?"

"Lorraine was thrown from a horse at Brighton Stables," Lisa explained.

Shanon went pale. "Is she going to be okay?"

"I think so. She's being checked out now. Amy and Palmer are with her," Lisa said reassuringly. "Murphy—I mean Lorraine—wants you to come to the infirmary as soon as possible."

Shanon nodded, turning away with a terse, "Be right back. I have to get my jacket."

Muffin shoved her hands in her pockets and dropped her gaze to the floor. "Shanon's got you for moral support, and for sure, Lorraine doesn't want me hanging around," she said. "I think I'll wait for you in 3-D."

"Okay," said Lisa. "See you later."

"See you," Muffin echoed forlornly.

On the way to the infirmary, Lisa filled Shanon in on the few details she knew about the mishap. "Late this morning, right after the accident, one of the guys from the stables took Lorraine to the hospital in Brighton. She never did see a doctor, though, because the emergency room was so crowded. She sat there for nearly five hours, then finally decided to take a taxi back to campus."

Shanon stopped short, her jaw dropping with surprise. A rapid glance at the clock in the chapel tower told her it had only been a little over three hours since she'd last seen her new roommate. At this point she had two choices: either blurt out the truth or keep her mouth shut. Since she didn't want to confirm Lisa's already biased view of Lorraine, she stayed silent.

When they arrived at the infirmary, Amy, Palmer, and Lorraine were just coming out. The redhead's face was ghostly pale and her forehead was creased with pain. Shanon's dark suspicion that Lorraine had lied about the entire incident was immediately laid to rest.

"Thanks for coming, Shanon," Lorraine said shakily, making an obvious effort to keep her bottom lip from trembling. "I've already caused Amy and Palmer far too much trouble. Would you mind helping me back to the dorm?"

Shanon slipped her arm around Lorraine's waist. "Sure thing."

As the two started slowly back across the quad, the taller girl was limping noticeably.

Lisa watched them leave, thoroughly confused. "Shouldn't Murphy have at least been kept in the infirmary overnight?"

"For what? Nurse Jackson examined her thoroughly, and she gave her a clean bill of health," Palmer reported.

"Except for a small bruise and a few scratches on her arm, you couldn't even tell she'd fallen," Amy added to the diagnosis.

"Well, the way she's acting, you'd think she'd broken every bone in her body," Lisa said.

Palmer snorted. "Acting is the operative word in that sentence. Someone should present Lorraine Murphy with an Oscar for her performance."

Amy was more charitable. "I don't think she's actually faking the whole thing." She exchanged a knowing glance with the others and added, "But something tells me she's going to get a whole lot of mileage out of this fall."

CHAPTER ELEVEN

Dear Amy,

I have a really embarrassing confession to make—although I wouldn't be surprised if you've already guessed it. You see, there really isn't any guy named X. I've been talking about myself all along.

It's hard to explain how I feel about Tricia, and you're the only person I'd even try it with. Every time I think of her, my knees feel like they're made of Silly Putty. And when I get a letter from her, I walk around all day with a stupid grin on my face. Do you think that means I'm in love? And after all the times she's dumped on me, am I an idiot to think she might really be interested in me now? I don't know the answers to any of those questions, and they're driving me crazy.

To top it all off, I feel like the world's biggest jerk—I should've been mature enough to tell you the truth from the beginning. I hope you aren't mad at me—and I'd still like to know what you think I should do. Please write soon.

Your friend,
John

Amy put down John's letter and looked up at her friends. There was a moment of stunned silence in 3-D. Then, after a collective gasp, three of the five girls seated in a circle on the floor began talking at once.

"How could we have been so dumb?" Lisa exclaimed. "We should have guessed John was talking about himself!"

"All this time, he's been involved with another girl," said Shanon. "I can't believe it!"

"John's a total rat," Palmer pronounced. "He doesn't deserve a terrific girl like you, Amy. If I were you, I'd write him a real 'Dear John' letter."

Amy stared down at the floor in confusion. She didn't know *what* to think. John's confession had been a major shock, but somehow the pity she saw reflected on her suitemates' faces was even harder to bear.

"Why are you all making such a big deal about this," she said, fighting back tears. "John's entitled to go out with anyone he wants. It's not as if we're going steady or anything. . . ." Her voice trailed off unhappily.

"That isn't the point," Lisa said, putting a consoling arm around Amy's shoulder. "He *lied* to you!"

"He's obviously been hooked on Tricia all along," Palmer joined in. "I say you should dump him—quick!"

"I don't know," Amy said doubtfully. All her friends seemed to think she should be mad at John. But she didn't *feel* mad. She felt . . . She didn't know *how* she felt.

Amy looked from Lisa to Palmer to Shanon. They all looked flushed and angry. Then she turned to the silent Muffin. Although she didn't expect much help from that quarter, she felt it only polite to ask, "What do *you* think about all this?"

Muffin's gaze was both startled and grateful. "John shouldn't have made up the fib," she began cautiously. She straightened her shoulders and her thin voice picked up confidence. "But I think it's really neat that he felt close enough to you to share his problems."

Amy's eyes widened in surprise, and a slow smile spread across her face. Muffin was right. John was a boy and he certainly was a friend, but that didn't make him her boyfriend. There'd never really been anything romantic between them. And she did value the trust he had given her. She reached out impulsively to clasp the other girl's hand. "Thanks, Muffin—I needed that."

"It's the most sensible and mature thing anybody's said so far," Shanon admitted. "Good for you, Muff!"

Palmer popped the top from a can of diet cola and raised the drink in a toast. "Let's hear it for Muffin!"

"It was nothing," Muffin protested modestly, glowing with the praise. "Now, since no one else has letters to read, will you all help me with my answer to Geordie?"

"I wouldn't be much good to you. I'm so tired I can hardly see straight." Shanon stood and stretched, adding, "Does anyone mind if I stay here and type a paper? Lorraine had another migraine, and any kind of noise gets on her nerves."

Palmer opened her mouth to protest, but Lisa elbowed her before she could blurt out a sarcastic comment.

"Of course we don't mind," Amy responded. "And as far as I'm concerned, this is still your home."

With a grateful smile, Shanon settled herself at the typewriter while the quartet on the floor got down to business.

"Okay, Muffin—read what you've got so far," Palmer said.

Dear Geordie,

I liked your letter very much, but I'm not at all like the mental picture you have of me. I'm the shortest girl in my class, I'm very shy, and I'm terrible at sports.

I do like hard crossword puzzles, though. I'm enclosing one from The New York Times *that you might enjoy.*

Sincerely,
Muffin Talbot

"It's good, but something's missing," Lisa said as tactfully as her impatience would allow. "For starters, the tone is too negative—you're putting yourself down again."

"I was only trying to be honest," Muffin said. "How would you have written it?"

"Hmmm." Lisa stared off into space, waiting for an inspiration. When it hit, she picked up a pen and wrote rapidly.

Dear Geordie,

Or do you prefer being called Sherlock Holmes? I hate to spoil your fun, but you've picked up a few wrong clues. Your mental picture of me isn't quite accurate—I actually write much taller than I am in person!

I haven't had a chance to rent the video you recommended, but I did check out a library book on football. Most of the stuff was a little too technical for me, so I made up my own definitions. Here are some examples:

"Red Dog"—a spicy Russian frankfurter.

"Blitz"—the nickname of one of Santa's reindeer.

"Fullback"—the sum of one halfback and two quarterbacks.

How am I doing so far? Ha-ha!

I admit that I'll never be a network sportscaster, but when it comes to crossword puzzles, I'm Super Bowl all the way. I'm sending you a copy of a crossword puzzle I cut out of The New York Times. *I finished all but one square in the northeast corner. Can you top that?*

Thanks for the picture. My friends agree that for an ordinary guy, you're pretty special. I look forward to your next letter.

> *Yours truly,*
> *Muffin*

"The football definitions are a bit much," Amy commented, twanging a sour chord on her guitar to emphasize the point.

Lisa started to cross out that passage in the letter, then thought better of it. "He likes humor," she protested. "Besides, I found them in a really funny joke book."

"Amy's right." Palmer glanced up from a fashion magazine she was reading. "I say get rid of all that juvenile sports stuff. The letter has to be more sophisticated and mysterious to keep an upperclassman interested."

"If you're such an expert," Lisa bristled, "why don't *you* write this letter?"

The clatter from the typewriter in the far corner of the suite stopped abruptly. Shanon ripped the sheet of paper from the roller and crumpled it into a ball. "Why don't you *all* butt out and let Muffin write her own letters," she broke in, raising her voice above the hubbub in the room. "And would you mind holding the noise down a little? I'm trying to work here."

Lisa swallowed a sharp retort and instead offered a brief

"Sorry!" Shanon had been extra touchy since Lorraine's accident.

"We can finish this some other time. I promised Brenda Smith I'd trim her bangs," Muffin said, jumping up from the floor.

Shanon's annoyance immediately faded. "Don't leave because of me. I didn't mean to yell like that," she apologized. "It's just kind of hard for me to concentrate with everyone talking at once."

"That's okay, Shanon," Amy said. "We know you're worried about that makeup math quiz next Monday. If it'll help, the four of us can pull an all-nighter. We'll drill you until numbers are coming out of your ears."

"I appreciate the thought, but right now I've got to finish typing this paper. Lorraine needs it by nine o'clock in the morning."

Palmer nearly choked on the soda she was drinking. "Did you just say what I thought you said?!" she exclaimed incredulously.

Lisa tossed her long, brown hair back, her expression disbelieving. "This may be a stupid question, Shanon, but why are you letting your own work slide while you're doing Murphy's?"

"Because she needs me, that's why," Shanon said simply. "She can't write or type because her wrist was injured when she fell from the horse." She fiddled with the stack of papers on the table for a moment before adding, "Besides, just typing the paper isn't all that bad. It's correcting the spelling and grammar that's taking so much time."

Amy sat bolt upright. "You mean you're actually *editing* the paper for Lorraine?"

Even Muffin couldn't contain her outrage. "Can't you see

that Lorraine is just using you?" she cried, her voice rising to an indignant squeak. Jumping up, she marched across the room to confront Shanon. "She's been giving you all sorts of presents lately, hasn't she?"

Shanon's hand automatically started toward the butterfly clip that held back her sandy hair, but then she self-consciously put her hand down.

"So what?" she said defensively.

"That's the way she hooks you. Can't you see what's going on here?" Lisa got up from the floor and began to pace. "You do a favor just to be helpful, then Murphy bribes you with a present. It keeps happening until pretty soon you feel that you really owe her. So you start running errands for her, and doing her homework."

"And making excuses for her," Amy interjected softly. "This afternoon, didn't you tell Mr. Griffith that Lorraine would be late for class because she had an appointment at the infirmary?"

Shanon felt a hot flush zip up her neck. "It was the truth," she insisted.

"Maybe—maybe not," Palmer said. "Murphy has been known to lie. For instance, when I passed her room this morning, her door was open and she was typing for all she was worth. And she didn't seem to be having one bit of trouble with her so-called injured wrist."

The picture her suitemates were painting was too close to reality for Shanon to ignore, but she still believed they were misjudging Lorraine. "You don't know her the way I do. Sure, she can be demanding, but she's sensitive and good-hearted, too. She's sure that nobody likes her, though, and she thinks that the only way to make friends is to give people things."

71

"Thank you for that excellent analysis, Dr. Freud," Palmer scoffed.

Lisa silenced her blond suitemate with a warning look, then turned to Shanon. "You may have a point," she admitted. "But you're still not going to straighten out Lorraine's life by being her 'gofer'—that just isn't what friendship is about. You've got to take care of your own problems first."

"That's great advice," Shanon said softly but firmly. "And I think I should use it right now." She looked around the big room, her gaze level. "First off, I want things the way they were—with the beds in the small rooms and the desk over by the window where I can study."

Muffin's face turned even paler than usual. "If we do that, I'll have to move in with Lorraine again," she protested.

"Sooner or later you've got to try settling your differences with her. I'm sure the two of you can work something out if you really want to," Shanon responded. "Since this is a democracy, I think we should take a vote. All in favor of going back to the old arrangement, raise your hands."

Palmer's shot up immediately. "That sounds good to me. Between Lisa's mumbling in her sleep and Muffin's nightlight, I haven't gotten a decent rest in weeks."

"That's because your own snoring keeps you awake," Lisa teased. "I say things are fine the way they are."

Amy hesitated for a moment. But then she took a deep breath and cast her ballot. "I really don't want to make you unhappy, Muffin, but if Shanon doesn't pull up her grades, she might lose her scholarship. I have to be on her side."

"Three to one—majority rules," Shanon tallied, feeling better than she had in a very long while. But some of her triumph evaporated when she saw the look of betrayal on Muffin's face.

"How could you do this to me? I thought you were my friends," Muffin said plaintively, her bottom lip trembling. But to her credit, she didn't shed a tear. Spinning quickly, she bolted from the suite.

"I'd better go after her," Lisa said.

"Me, too. It's my fault she's so upset," Shanon insisted, close on Lisa's heels.

"I knew Shanon would come around," Amy said to Palmer after the others had gone. "She's too sensitive herself not to see Muffin's side of things," she added softly, her face thoughtful.

"They're both a little too sensitive for their own good if you ask me," Palmer said. "Anyway, all this drama has made me hungry. I think I'll hit the snack bar for some ice cream. Want to come along?"

"I've got something I want to do first," Amy answered. "I'll meet you there in a little while."

Dear John,

I can understand why you were embarrassed to admit that you were Mr. X, but no, I'm not mad. What's important is that you had enough trust in me to share your problems. Unfortunately, I'm afraid I don't have any good answers to your questions. It's hard for me to really understand your feelings for Tricia, because I've never felt that way about anybody.

There's one thing I do know, though—you owe it to yourself to find out what Tricia really means to you. I don't think writing is enough in this case. You need to see her face-to-face and talk honestly about your relationship.

Be sure to let me know how the visit turns out. And remember, I'm in there rooting for you no matter what.

Your friend,
Amy

CHAPTER TWELVE

———◆———

Dear Rob,

We've re-rearranged the suite again so that everything is the way it was before. So much for the grand experiment in interior decorating! I can't admit this to Shanon, Palmer, and Amy, but I'm glad 3-D is back to normal.

Muffin was pretty upset about leaving the suite, but at least she doesn't have to share a room with Murphy anymore. Luckily, a triple down the hall had an unexpected vacancy, and we talked Miss Grayson into giving it to Muffin. We also convinced Muff it was time to give up her pink curtains and the night-light (her new roommates are very relieved). She and Shanon made up after their disagreement, so she still spends a lot of time here with us.

Those are the major happenings in Fox Hall. What's going on at Ardsley these days? I know you must be busy, but as soon as you can squeeze out a few extra minutes, I'd love to hear all the juicy details. Don't take this as a complaint, but your last few letters have been kind of short. I really want to hear how you're doing.

Lisa

P.S. Muffin's still very shy when it comes to her pen pal relationship with Geordie Randolph. I think it would help a lot if she could talk to him in person. The Foxes all have shopping passes into Brighton next Saturday—Muffin, too. Do you think you and the guys could get Geordie to meet us at Figaro's? I'll try to time things so that we hit the pizza parlor around two. Please, please try to make it. Not only for Muffin's sake, either—I'd really like to see you.

Dear Mars,

Send me a "high five" by express mail—I aced Mrs. Terwilliger's makeup math quiz! And I'm doing much better in art, too. I took your advice and went the abstract route. For the sky of my painting, I dumped lots of pastel colors on a canvas and swirled them around like marble cake. Then I used my elbow to make tree trunks and dabbed on leaves with my fingertips. I call my masterpiece "Dreamscape," and my teacher says it's very imaginative. It'll never hang in the Met, but I did get a B plus for it!

There's only one problem: Now that things are going so much better for me, I feel kind of guilty about Lorraine. She doesn't have a roommate now, and she says she prefers it that way, but I still visit her a lot because I know she's very lonely. After her parents' divorce, her mother remarried and moved to Paris. Lorraine never hears from her. And although her father sends her lots of expensive things, he never bothers to write either. I hate to imagine how hard it must be to have folks who don't care about you. I'm so glad I have such a warm, close family.

While we're on the the subject of families, I have to tell you about my latest project. Mr. Griffith assigned our cre-

ative writing class an essay on the subject, "Who Am I in the Eyes of My Family?" We're talking about a major paper here—it'll count for one-third of my final grade. For research, I wrote all the members of my family—even the aunts, uncles, and cousins—and asked them each to send back a one-word description of my personality. Just for kicks, would you do it, too? I'd love to find out what my pen pal really thinks of me.

Thanks again for helping me over the rough spots. I don't know what I would have done without you.

Truly, truly, truly yours,
Shanon

"You certainly hit the jackpot today. Are all those from your pen pal?" Lorraine asked, coming up behind Shanon outside of Booth Hall.

"No, they're from my family," Shanon replied. Grinning jubilantly, she shuffled through the thick bundle of letters she had just pulled from her mailbox. It had been less than a week since she wrote to her family, and already the answers were pouring in.

"What a haul!" Shanon exclaimed. "Here's one from Aunt Dottie in Des Moines, and I didn't even write to her. Grandma Davis must have phoned her about my research."

"What research?" Lorraine asked, eyeing the envelopes curiously.

"For the essay Mr. Griffith assigned in English," Shanon explained, stuffing the loot in her bookbag.

"Yuk!" Lorraine's pretty features registered disgust. " 'Who Am I in the Eyes of My Family?'—what a drippy topic! There must be a billion things to write about that would be more important and interesting."

"Offhand, I can't think of one," Shanon said, still smiling. "Have you started your paper yet?"

"I've jotted down a few notes. I was just heading for the library to do some more digging," the redhead said vaguely. "Want to walk me over? On the way, you could tell me about your research."

No thanks, was on the tip of Shanon's tongue, but the forlorn look on Lorraine's face changed it to, "Sure, I'd be glad to."

The afternoon sky outside was a clean, clear blue, the air fresh with the promise of an early spring. But Shanon was so excited about her project, she scarcely noticed the balmy day.

". . . So I asked everyone to send a one-word description of me." She filled in the details of her idea as they strolled across the quad.

"Clever," Lorraine commented. Her gray eyes held a mixture of admiration and some emotion Shanon couldn't identify. Stopping at a stone bench beside the gravel path, she plopped down with a wistful, "I bet your relatives have all sorts of good things to say about you."

"We could read a couple of the letters now if you have time," Shanon said, taking a seat beside Lorraine.

"That's a cute idea."

My dearest Shanon,

To me, you're a Golden Delicious apple: *pretty on the outside and sweet down to the very core.*

Hugs and kisses,
Nana

"Trust Grandma Davis to mention food—cooking is her

78

life. And Granny Hughes will probably call me her cuddly ball of yarn. She's the artsy-craftsy type," Shanon explained, smiling. "What are your grandmothers like, Lorraine?"

"One's the wicked witch of the west, and the other's in a nursing home," was the chilling response.

"Oh." Shanon squirmed uncomfortably and tore open the next envelope.

Hello, Snickerdoodle!
The word that fits you best is mischievous. *I'll never forget the time you snitched your Uncle Harry's toupee and used it to make a bear-skin rug for your dollhouse.*

> *Stay sweet and keep out of trouble,*
> *Auntie Zelda*

Lorraine opened the notebook she was carrying and absently began to doodle. "I bet your uncle was furious with you for pulling that stunt."

"Actually, he thought it was hilarious. He said the hair looked better in my doll's living room than it did on his head," Shanon giggled.

Yo, Pee Wee!
When I read your letter, the first word that popped into my head was ears. *You're a first-rate listener. Come home soon for a visit. Believe it or not, I miss you.*

> *Your big sis,*
> *Doreen*

Hi, Sweets,
To borrow a line from a song, you are the sunshine *of my*

life. Your smile starts my day and makes flowers grow in my heart.

> *I love you very much,*
> *Mom*

Little Girl,
  You're so many things to me that I can't think of any one word that fits you. All I can say is that you make your old man proud.

> *Love,*
> *Dad*

"You probably have no idea how lucky you are." Lorraine's tone was harsh, accusing.

"Is something wrong?" Shanon queried, startled by the sudden anger she heard in the other girl's voice.

"As a matter of fact, everything's peachy keen. Now I know exactly how to write that stupid essay." Lorraine penciled some strokes in her notebook. Then, ripping out the sheet of paper, she dropped it in Shanon's lap. "That's who *I* am in the eyes of *my* family," she rasped. And jumping to her feet, she ran the rest of the way to the library without a backward look.

Shanon stared down at the paper, her eyes misting with pity.

The one word on the page was: *nobody.*

CHAPTER THIRTEEN

"That lemon-yellow jumpsuit is perfect," Shanon sighed. She pressed closer to the window of the Strawberry Fields Boutique for a better look. "I'm going to ask Mom to make me one just like it."

"Ooooh, look at the swimsuits," Muffin directed, moving on to the next display.

"The two-piece turquoise one would look great on you, Palmer," Amy commented. "Want to go in and try it on?"

Palmer wrinkled her noise in disdain. "No thanks. I don't want anything from this hick store—next month Mother's taking me to New York to pick out my whole summer wardrobe!"

"Well, excuse me!" Amy lifted one eyebrow. "I'm surprised you're not popping over to France on the Concorde."

"What a fabulous suggestion!" Palmer clasped her hands in ecstasy, her eyes taking on a dreamy glow. "Paris in the spring . . . the Champs Élysées . . . chestnuts blossoming . . ."

"The only chestnuts you'll be dealing with are the ones rattling around in your head," Lisa teased, giggling. She shifted the bag containing the nightgown she'd just bought and glanced at her wristwatch. She hadn't told any of the others about the meeting she and Rob had arranged at the pizza parlor, and she was very nervous about it. "We've still got over an hour before we're due back on campus. How about stopping off at Figaro's for a Monstro?"

"Great idea!" Amy said eagerly. "I'm starved."

As usual on Saturday afternoons, Brighton's favorite teen hangout was packed to the rafters. Music videos flickered on the jumbo TV screen and the air vibrated with a heavy metal beat. The girls placed their order at the front counter, then moved to a clear space beside the door to wait.

"It'll be at least half an hour before we can get a table," Amy said, raising her voice to be heard above the noise.

"Let's just get takeouts," Palmer suggested.

"We can't! The pizza would be cold and rubbery by the time we got back to Alma," Lisa insisted. She didn't want the other girls' impatience to spoil her carefully planned scheme to throw Muffin and Geordie together. She scanned the crowd anxiously, her stomach flipping a double somersault as a familiar figure got up from a table across the room. "Hey, look—it's Rob!" she cried as he waved at them.

Shanon squealed her delight. "And Mars!"

"John's with them, too!" Amy announced with a broad grin.

Palmer's eyes widened as she studied the fourth guy at the table. He was tall and handsome, and a sun-streaked cowlick fell over his forehead. "Isn't that—"

"G-Geordie Randolph. I r-recognize him from the p-picture," Muffin stammered. Cheeks flaming, she began inching her way toward the door. "I think I'd b-better get b-back to school. I've got to wash my hair."

"Oh, no you don't! You're going to meet your pen pal if I have to drag you over there." Lisa snagged the shy girl's arm and steered her toward the boys. Halfway across the crowded room, the panicked Muffin tried to bolt, nearly colliding with a passing waiter. Lisa tightened her grasp and muttered, "Don't even think about chickening out on this."

"But I won't know what to say to him," Muffin protested.

"Don't sweat it, I'll coach you," Palmer offered blandly.

The guys quickly appropriated five chairs from neighboring tables, jamming them into a close circle around their own.

"It's been a long time since we all got together," Mars said, guiding Shanon to a seat beside his.

"At least a century," she agreed. "If it hadn't been for your help, I don't think I would've made it through the past few weeks."

"Oh, I don't know," he said, tweaking the tip of her nose. "You're pretty tough. But I'm glad I was able to help."

"Hi, Amy," John said. Avoiding her gaze, he shoved the remains of a pizza aside to make room for her packages.

"Say hello to Geordie Randolph, everyone." Rob went on to give the upperclassman a rundown on the members of the group: "Shanon, Palmer, Amy, and last but definitely not least—Lisa McGreevy!" he finished with a proprietary grin.

Lisa flushed with a mixture of pleasure and embarrassment. "Hi, Geordie." She nodded at the football player, then nudged the fifth girl forward. "Meet Muffin Talbot, your pen pal."

Geordie extended his hand, his smile showcasing dazzling

dimples and perfect white teeth. "It's great to meet you, Muffin. I told my teammates your football jokes, and they all cracked up. Your write terrific letters."

"Thanks a lot. I'm glad—" Lisa blurted out before she could stop herself. Color deepening, she moved on to cover the blunder; "That is—er, Muffin is glad you like them."

Rob shot Lisa a curious look as she settled happily beside him, but he didn't comment. "This was a great idea," he said instead. And, draping one arm casually over the back of her chair, he added, "I've really missed you."

"Me, too. Thanks for helping me put this together," she whispered, all too conscious of his fingers grazing her shoulder. She glanced up to meet his gaze, her heart thudding rapidly against her rib cage. She'd forgotten how thick and silky his eyelashes were. Suddenly it didn't matter at all that his letters had been a bit stale and routine lately. In person, he was absolutely wonderful.

"What do you think of our good buddy Geordie?" Rob leaned over to ask in a low tone.

"He's okay," Lisa replied offhandedly. She slid a look to the other side of the table where Geordie was flanked by Palmer and Muffin. The upperclassman was dividing his attention equally between them in spite of the fact that Palmer was making an obvious play for him. "And he's being very nice to Muffin. In my book, that's a definite plus."

"I was kind of surprised when I first saw her," Rob confided. "She's really shy, isn't she? I was expecting a real tiger from the way G.R. described her letters."

"You haven't actually read any of them, have you?" Lisa asked anxiously.

"Nope. We guys talk about you girls a lot, but we usually don't compare notes."

Relief made her giddy. Rob would surely have recognized her handwriting on Muffin's supposed correspondence. "Good policy," she murmured. The next 3-D gabfest was going to be an interesting one, she thought, wondering idly what the other girls would have to report.

In Amy's case, it wouldn't be much. "Did that girl, uh, your friend Tricia, visit last weekend?" she finally broke the strained silence that hung between her and John.

He ducked his head, busying himself with the ice cubes melting in his soda glass. "Uh-huh," he grunted.

"Did she—was it—I mean—how did it go?"

John hesitated, glancing warily around the table. "I'd rather not say just yet. I'll write to you about it."

"Fine," Amy said, hurt by the distance in his eyes. He could tell me now, if he really wanted to, she thought dejectedly. It wasn't as though the other couples would have overheard the conversation—they were all too wrapped up in each other to care.

"I'd better go see if your orders are ready," John said, rising abruptly.

"Rob and I will clear the table, then we'll give you a hand with the trays," Mars offered.

Rob reluctantly rose from his seat. "Don't wander off," he cautioned Lisa with a smile.

Geordie was halfway up when Palmer caught his arm. "They can handle it. You haven't finished telling Muffin and me about San Diego," she cooed.

"It's a good thing we're not in the desert," Lisa leaned over to whisper to Shanon. "Palmer is batting her lashes hard enough to whip up a sandstorm."

"I don't think Geordie's interested though. He really seems to like Muffin," Shanon said.

To their disappointment, the three pen pals from Ardsley didn't sit down again when they returned with the food. "We hate to break this up, but we've got to get back to Ard-barf," John explained, retrieving his jacket.

" 'Bye," Amy muttered without looking at him.

Rob bent down and gently tugged Lisa's hair. "I'll write you as soon as I get back to the dorm."

"I bet our letters will cross in the mail," she said happily.

Then Geordie got up, holding out one hand to Muffin, the other to Palmer. "It's been a pleasure meeting you. Let's do this again real soon."

As soon as the boys were out the door, Muffin threw her arms around Lisa. "That Geordie is so adorable," she squeaked, "and he's *sooooo* intelligent. He has a photographic memory and he knows lots about English literature. He and his uncle in San Diego played Jeopardy all the time while they worked on the boat, and Geordie always won the poetry categories."

"Forget the poetry, his uncle has a boat!" Palmer chimed in.

She seemed as interested in Geordie as Muffin—maybe more, Lisa thought, alarm bells going off in her head. "That's good to know, Muff. You can throw a couple of quotes into your next letter," she suggested, ignoring Palmer's comment. "I'll help you—"

"Let's carry the pizza back to the dorm," Amy broke in, already getting to her feet. "It's too crowded in here, and the noise is giving me a headache."

"Good plan," Shanon said gently.

The other girls caught onto Amy's mood swing immediately—all except Palmer, who was too busy fantasizing about Geordie Randolph to pay much attention. She was much more his type than shy, little Muffin, she decided. Next year, as captain of the football team, he'd need to date a girl with style and pizzazz. Someone sophisticated, who matched his blond good looks. It didn't take long for her to nominate the ideal candidate: Palmer Durand!

Now all that remained was to get Geordie's vote. By the time the group trooped out of Figaro's, Palmer was already plotting the perfect campaign strategy.

CHAPTER FOURTEEN

Dear Geordie,
  This is the answer:

> *"She walks in beauty, like the night*
> *Of cloudless climes and starry skies;*
> *And all that's best of dark and bright*
> *Meet in her aspect and her eyes...."*

If you try very hard, I'm sure you'll be able to come up with the question.

Your Unknown Pen Pal
P.S. I'll give you a hint—think of someone the quote describes perfectly!

"Tolstoy wrote *War and Peace* in less time than it's taking you to finish that letter," Amy teased, glancing at her watch.

"What?" Startled, Palmer jerked her attention away from the leather portfolio in front of her.

"You haven't written Sam in such a long time, I guess you've got a lot to say," Lisa said good-naturedly.

"Sam?" Palmer echoed, her blue eyes blank for a split second. "Oh, right. Uh, I was—uh—just telling him, I mean—saying how much his song—uh—meant," she babbled.

Lisa eyed her quizzically. "Are you okay?" she asked. "Your face is all red."

"I'm fine," Palmer shot back, slapping her folder shut. "It's just a little warm in here."

Shanon sauntered over to the desk and picked up the book beside Palmer's elbow. "Hmmm, *Passages from the Masters of English Poetry*," she read the title aloud. "This is pretty heavy stuff. Where'd you get it?"

"If you must know, I borrowed it from Mr. Griffith. I—I'm doing an assignment for extra credit," she said in a rush. "Come on," she urged, "we'd better get a move on if we don't want to miss lunch."

Mrs. Butter had been on a seafood binge all week: Dover sole, salmon salad, and the ever-popular fish and chips. The special for the fourth day was a scrumptious-looking but decidedly fishy-smelling casserole.

"Pretty soon, we're going to sprout fins," Shanon predicted.

"I love scallops in cream sauce," Palmer said as she sampled the portion on her plate. "I wouldn't mind a few more shrimps, though."

"Hurry up and finish," Amy commanded. "The mail is due any minute. If we hurry, we can stop off at Booth Hall on our way to the science lab."

A knowing look passed among the other three. Amy hadn't heard from John since the meeting in Figaro's.

"Are you enjoying Lord Byron, Palmer?" a deep voice broke the silence. Mr. Griffith, their English teacher and not-so-secret heartthrob, stopped at their table with his tray.

"He's absolutely dreamy," Palmer gushed. Shanon smiled to herself as she wondered whether her suitemate meant the poet or the professor. "Actually," Palmer went on, "we were just discussing the English influence on life in America."

"She means we were talking about Mrs. Butter's special," Amy translated. "Won't you join us?"

"Thanks, but I'll have to take a rain check." The glint of amusement in Mr. Griffith's eyes faded as he shifted his attention. "I just stopped by to ask you to come to my office this afternoon, Shanon. I'd like to discuss your essay with you."

"I'd be glad to," she responded.

"Well, then, I'll see you around four."

As he strode away, Shanon looked after him with a worried frown. "He seemed so serious. I hope he isn't going to say he hated my paper."

"Probably just the opposite. He probably wants to enter it in some contest," Lisa reassured her.

Palmer drained the milk in her glass, then delicately dabbed her lips with her napkin. "I told you you should've discussed the idea with him before you wrote the essay," she reproved.

"I wanted to surprise him." Shanon's worry was rapidly escalating into a full-blown anxiety attack. "Maybe he's going to deduct points because I turned it in an hour after the deadline."

"There are no 'maybes' about it. Your family essay was terrific, Mr. Griffith adored it, and you racked up an A plus," Amy firmly ended the speculation. "Now can we go pick up the mail?"

But she was to be disappointed again: all of the boxes were empty, except for Lisa's.

Dear Lisa,

Our history class has been studying the French Revolution, and I came up with a brilliant plan: Since we'll be on summer vacation by July 14th, I suggested that Ardsley observe Bastille Day in April. The idea really took off—the heads of our history and French departments are going to meet with the teachers at Alma to coordinate a joint celebration!

I must admit I had an ulterior motive for pushing the plan. It's another chance for us to get together. I know it's still a long time away, but, Mademoiselle McGreevy, will you be my date?

Répondez s'il vous plaît!

Votre ami,
Rob

P.S. Geordie Randolph has been getting the most incredible letters from some girl at Alma who signs herself "The Unknown Pen Pal." They're sprayed with perfume and so hot it's a wonder they don't set the postman's bag on fire. Geordie is dying to answer, but there's never a dorm address on the envelopes. They definitely don't sound like Muffin's style. Do you have any idea who G.R.'s mystery lady could be?

"Don't look at me," Amy sighed when Lisa had finished reading. She strummed a series of doleful minor chords on her guitar, adding, "I'm already having trouble with one pen pal—I have no desire to get involved with another."

"Geordie's a hunk, but I prefer good old Mars," Shanon said, smiling.

"What about you, Palmer?" Lisa said slyly. "Those letters may not sound like Muffin, but they sure sound like you!"

Her blond suitemate was all wide-eyed innocence. "What's the point of writing someone and not including a return address?" was her careless response.

"Good question," Lisa agreed. She straightened abruptly, her eyes glinting with a sudden suspicion. "Muffin told me that Murphy used to go through her mail. I'll bet you anything the Unknown Pen Pal is Lorraine!"

"I don't believe that," Shanon automatically came to Lorraine's defense.

Lisa shrugged and, not wanting to start a fight, dropped the subject. Pulling out her box of pale yellow stationery, she plopped down on the loveseat and prepared to write.

"I see you're not wasting any time accepting Rob's invitation," Amy teased.

"I don't want to give him a chance to change his mind," Lisa murmured, grinning. She scribbled for a moment, then raised her head, obviously pleased with herself. "This line sounds so good I think I'll use it in Muffin's letter to Geordie, too."

Whenever I'm depressed, I close my eyes and remember the things you said at Figaro's. And voilà! *The clouds in my world drift away.*

"That isn't at all the sort of stuff Muffin would say to Geordie," Shanon pointed out.

"She would if she could get up the nerve," Lisa insisted.

"I think it's time we let Muffin handle her own pen pal relationship," Amy warned. "It's dishonest for you to keep writing to Geordie."

"So do I," Lisa admitted sheepishly. "But this is absolutely the last time. From here on, Muffin is strictly on her own."

Quickly finishing Rob's letter, she pulled out a sheet of the pink paper Muffin had provided. With the out-takes she'd saved from her own correspondence, she made short work of the letter to Geordie. But before she could sign the M. with her usual flourish, a shrill alarm bell sounded.

"I detest fire drills," Palmer complained, nevertheless jumping up and struggling into her jacket.

Amy followed suit, and the two dashed out into the hallway.

Shanon hesitated at the door of Suite 3-D, looking back at her roommate. "If you don't want to get three demerits, you'd better hurry, Lisa."

"I might as well mail these while I'm out," Lisa said, hurriedly addressing two envelopes. In her haste to leave, she didn't notice that she had stuffed the pink letter in the yellow envelope and vice-versa.

It wasn't until Rob's answer arrived three days later that she realized her horrible mistake.

Lisa,

Or should I call you the Unknown Pen Pal? I just wanted to assure you that Geordie got your last letter. The reason I know is that I delivered it in person! He gave me the one that was meant for me, but I tore it up when I noticed you'd used the same stale lines on both of us.

93

If you were interested in G.R., all you had to do was say so, and I would've backed off. I hate stupid mind games, and I don't care very much for people who play them.

Au revoir, Mam'selle McGreevy—in case you haven't heard, that's French for "You're history."

Rob Williams

Dear Mars,

This is absolutely, positively the worst week of my whole, entire life! When I went to Mr. Griffith's office, he said that some of the things I wrote in my essay were almost identical to those in another student's paper. And guess what? The other girl was Lorraine Murphy!

Mr. Griffith actually accused me of copying her idea. The weird thing is, he didn't even seem mad—just disappointed in me. He kept saying that he wouldn't believe I'd do such a thing, but it was obvious he did believe it! I was so upset and hurt that I couldn't say a word. He and Miss Grayson are going to have another conference with me next week before he takes up the matter with our headmistress, Miss Pryn.

It's hard for me to understand why Lorraine would stab me in the back like this. She once told me I was the only real friend she'd ever had. Right now, I'm so confused.

How do you think I should handle this? Please answer right away. I'm desperate.

Shanon

CHAPTER FIFTEEN

———————◆———————

Dear Shanon,
  I think you're confused because you still like Lorraine and don't want to get her in trouble. But face it—your only option is to blow that liar out of the water! Go into that conference and defend yourself with all the ammunition you've got.
  Keep smiling. Remember, you've got the truth on your side.

                                        Love,
                                        Mars

"Try this, Shanon." Muffin offered her a pink angora sweater with a wide lace collar, confiding, "When I put this on, my mom calls me her little angel."

"You'll need my pearls, too," Palmer said. "I always wear them when I'm going for the innocent look."

"Personally, I think you should stick with the gray suit—straightforward and businesslike all the way," Lisa chimed in.

Shanon waved the advice aside. "Clothes aren't going to

impress Mr. Griffith and Miss Grayson. It's what I have to say that matters."

"Which is?" Amy asked gently.

"That this is all some horrible misunderstanding. I'll simply tell them that I talked with Lorraine about the idea, and that she probably just forgot where she heard it. I'm sure she wouldn't have stolen it deliberately."

Lisa gave Shanon a disbelieving look, but held her tongue as the accused grabbed a yellow slicker off the coat rack and slipped it on. "As much as I appreciate all your help, I think I need to be by myself for a while. I'm going for a walk before the conference."

As the door to 3-D closed behind Shanon, Muffin said, "I wish my dad were here. He's a lawyer, and I'm sure he could prove she's not guilty."

"Proof! That's it! The letters from Shanon's family!" Lisa's sagging shoulders straightened abruptly as a sudden gleam lit her eyes. "That's all the proof we need. Come on, gang—*we're* going to present Shanon's case."

Five minutes after the conference started Shanon knew her "there's-been-a-misunderstanding" defense wasn't going to wash.

"I'm sorry, Shanon, but Lorraine outlined the idea for me the week after I made the assignment," Mr. Griffith pointed out. "And she turned in her paper three days early," he added, looking almost as upset as Shanon felt.

A quick mental calculation told Shanon that Lorraine must have gone to Mr. Griffith right after she read the Davis family's letters. "It's possible for two people to have the same idea," she tried again.

"That's right, but they usually express it differently,"

Miss Grayson said, giving Shanon a searching look. "Mrs. Terwilliger told me you've been having problems lately. You're a very good student—and a very good person. I'm sure you wouldn't have cheated unless you were under extreme pressure."

"I wouldn't cheat no matter what!" Shanon insisted.

"We'd like to believe that, Shanon," Mr. Griffith put in, "but the similarities between your paper and Lorraine's can hardly be a coincidence. Take a look," he said gravely, handing her a sheet of loose-leaf paper. "This is from Lorraine's essay. Please read the section I've underlined, then tell me what you think."

My Aunt Zenobia calls me mischievous because when I was five, I snitched Uncle Harold's toupee and made a bear-skin rug for my dollhouse.

Shanon's face burned. Not only had Lorraine taken her idea, she'd actually stolen her family memories! Suddenly all of Shanon's uncertainties disappeared. Before she could stop herself, the entire story came pouring out—the bribery, the manipulations, the errands she'd run—even the excuses she'd been talked into making for Lorraine. When she was finished, the two teachers exchanged a significant glance.

"Those are very serious accusations, Shanon," Miss Grayson said gently. "I assume you have proof to back them up."

Before Shanon could answer, the office door swung open to admit a grim-faced delegation of four.

Mr. Griffith rose from his seat, frowning. "This is a private conference, girls. What we're discussing doesn't concern you."

"I—I—we're sorry, Mr. Griffith," Lisa blurted out. "But it does concern us. Our friend's entire future is on the line."

"We don't have any proof that Lorraine's aunt and uncle are imaginary," Amy piped up, "but it should be easy enough for you to check her family tree. And while you're at it, you should also take a look at the records from the last school she attended. Kate Ma—"

Lisa jabbed her elbow into Amy's ribs, cutting short the revelation. "A very reliable source told us that this isn't the first time Lorraine Murphy's been involved in an incident like this," she finished. Moving toward the desk, she laid the manila folder she was carrying in front of Mr. Griffith. "These are all the one-word descriptions Shanon's family sent her. If you look at the postmarks on the letters, you can easily check to see if they arrived *before* Lorraine started her essay."

"One more thing." Muffin stepped forward, her face red but her voice strong and steady. "If Shanon gets expelled, we're all leaving, too."

As Mr. Griffith leafed through the letters, a look of dismay flashed across his face. "No one said anything about expelling anyone," he said. "Your teacher should've done his homework, Shanon," he added contritely. "I'm sorry to have accused you without looking more deeply into the matter."

"That's okay," Shanon said quickly. "Lorraine fooled me, too." She looked at him, her face strained. "What's going to happen to her now?"

"That's something Miss Pryn will have to decide. As far as you girls are concerned, though, the case is closed," Mr. Griffith dismissed them with a smile.

When they were safely outside of the building, Shanon let

her relief show in a jubilant whoop. "You guys are the greatest!" she said, wrapping her arms around each of her suitemates in turn. "You, too, Muffin," she added. "You were a real tiger in there."

"I know," Muffin shot back. "Sometimes you just have to speak up!"

CHAPTER SIXTEEN

Dear John,
  I can't understand why you haven't written me. I thought things were so cool between us—

Dear John,
  I guess you and Tricia decided to get together. I hope you'll be very happy—

Dear John,
  This is a song I wrote to tell you how I feel.

  The sun never smiles through my window anymore.
  It's moved on to a new horizon.
  The flowers here are dying 'cause the light is gone
  And the birds have forgotten all their songs.
  I hate the darkness.
  It hurts so much to be alone—

Amy grimaced and ripped the page from her pad. After crumpling it into a ball, she tossed it toward the wastebasket. But it bounced off the rim, landing on the floor.

"Air ball!" Palmer ruled. "That's the third time you've missed the hoop, hotshot."

"Leave her alone, Palmer," Lisa warned. Retrieving the page, she rapidly scanned the lines. "This is pretty good, Amy. How come you're not sending it to John?"

"Because . . . he's probably too busy with Tricia to read it," Amy began hesitantly. The rest came out in an unhappy rush. "And because I've got too much pride. I don't want him to know how much I miss him."

"I wish we could think of some way to make you feel better," Shanon said, giving her a quick hug.

"I'll get over it sooner or later," Amy said bravely. "Speaking of downers, how's your apology going, Lisa?"

"It's not easy, but I think I've got it now," she replied. "Listen to this."

Dear Rob,

I know you're very angry with me, but at least let me tell you my side of the story. I started helping Muffin with her letters to Geordie Randolph because she didn't have enough confidence to do them alone. The first time she kind of told me what she wanted to say, and then I just spiced it up a bit. Geordie would have noticed if there had been two different types of handwriting, so after I wrote the first one, I was stuck with the job. The switch was a dumb mistake, and I can't tell you how sorry I am that it happened.

You have to believe me, though, when I tell you I am not—repeat—NOT the Unknown Pen Pal. In the first place, I think anonymous love letters are stupid. Second, although G.R. is very nice, I'm not the least bit interested in him. You're the only pen pal I want.

Please forgive me. I never intended to hurt your feelings. I hope you'll write me soon to say that everything's okay again.

Always,
Lisa

"That should do the trick," Palmer said approvingly.

"Maybe, maybe not. The mix-up was bad enough, but he's really mad because he thinks I'm one who sent Geordie those secret love notes," Lisa said.

"Do you still think the Unknown Pen Pal is Lorraine?" Amy asked.

"It wouldn't surprise me a bit," Lisa replied.

"I guess nothing about Lorraine could surprise me now," Shanon admitted, "but the theory still doesn't feel quite right to me."

"Well, I don't know," Lisa said angrily. "But if I ever find out who that sneak is, I'll—"

"It's not Lorraine's fault," Palmer broke in, running her finger nervously around the collar of her cashmere sweater.

"I don't know why you would defend a person who's too dishonest to sign her own name." A disturbing possibility narrowed Lisa's eyes, and she added an ominous, "Unless you know her very, very well."

Palmer began fiddling with her pearls as two bright pink spots appeared on her cheeks.

"It's you," Amy said at the same time that Shanon gasped, "Palmer's the Unknown Pen Pal!"

"I should have known you weren't really reading poetry for extra credit. You've been copying hot passages from Mr. Griffith's book and sending them to Geordie Randolph, haven't you?" Lisa accused.

"So what if I have?" Palmer mumbled. "You can't blame me for your problems, Lisa. I didn't switch the letters—you did."

"As much as I hate to admit it, she's right," Shanon said. "Calm down, Lisa. Getting mad at Palmer won't solve anything."

"No, but it will make me feel a heck of a lot better," Lisa snapped. "What are you trying to do, Palmer, set a world's record for collecting pen pals? You started off with John, then stole Simmie, dumped him, and got Sam. What do you need Geordie for?"

"He's really cute, and I've got a serious crush on him," Palmer responded with a helpless shrug.

"So does Muffin," Amy reminded her.

"Show me the rule book that says two people can't like the same boy," Palmer challenged. "I'm sure Geordie loves getting letters from more than one pen pal."

"What I can't understand is why you didn't sign your own name," Shanon said. "And why didn't you put a return address on the envelopes?"

"That was all part of my master plan," Palmer explained eagerly. "Geordie wasn't exactly overwhelmed by me when we were at Figaro's, so I had to do something creative to intrigue him. I borrowed Lisa's suggestion about sending him poetic quotes, and now he's dying to know who I am." Palmer sat down at the desk, surveying the others as though they were her pupils. "Phase two of the operation is to reveal my true identity. Do you want to hear the letter I just wrote him?"

"Not particularly," Amy said. "What do you intend to do about Sam? He likes you a lot. It would be really mean to dump him now."

"I wouldn't do that." For the first time since the discussion began, Palmer looked both guilty and uncomfortable. "Sam wouldn't mind a bit if he knew I was Geordie's pen pal, though. And besides, he doesn't even go to Ardsley anymore, so there's no chance he'll find out."

"Unless you tell him," Shanon prompted.

"Maybe I will—someday."

"I have a feeling we're wasting our breath," Lisa told Palmer. "You're going to do as you please no matter what we say." She plopped down on the floor, curiosity overcoming criticism. "Okay, go ahead. We might as well hear this brilliant letter!"

Dear Geordie,
  The final question in our Pen Pal Poetry Contest is:

> *"What's in a name? That which we call a rose*
> *By any other name would smell as sweet."*

If you guessed that Shakespeare is the author of the quote, and that it came from Romeo and Juliet, *you're the lucky winner!*

First prize is a five-by-seven photograph (suitable for framing) of your Unknown Pen Pal, also known as— Ta-dah!—PALMER DURAND!

My return address is on the envelope. Now that you know how to reach me, we can move on to the next exciting episode of the game. Looking forward to hearing from you!

            Yours very, very truly,
            Palmer

"I think I'm going to be sick," Amy groaned, clutching her stomach dramatically. "You've really hit a new low in insincerity, Palmer. I just hope Geordie won't be dumb enough to fall for that cutesy come-on."

"Me, too," Lisa said. "If he does, poor Muffin will be crushed. I hate to think how she's going to react when she finds out about it."

"Something tells me Muffin will survive," Shanon mused aloud. "Who knows? She may even be able to give Palmer some stiff competition."

CHAPTER SEVENTEEN

Dear Mars,

For a change, I've got terrific news. After all the upsetting stuff that's been going on, Mom and Dad think I need some rest and relaxation. They've arranged for me to come home for a three-day vacation, and get this—the rest of the Foxes are invited, too!

We could all use a change of scene, particularly Amy and Lisa. They're bummed out because John and Rob haven't written. Some assistance from my favorite "Mr. Fixit" wouldn't hurt—hint, hint! In other words, please see if you can nudge the guys a little.

I know I've already thanked you for helping me through the "Murphy" crisis, but I'd like to say it again. Thanks! I really treasure your friendship.

I'll write to you as soon as I get back from my mini vacation.

Love,
Shanon

"Come on, everybody, we're going for a holiday, not a

funeral," Shanon encouraged the troops as they stacked their knapsacks by the door of Suite 3-D. But her efforts did little to lift Amy's gloom. And Lisa's smile was clearly strained.

Even Palmer looked a little less cool than usual. "I should be taking my hair dryer," she fretted.

"Doreen will let you use hers," Shanon said. She glanced at her watch and frowned. "My dad will be picking us up in an hour or so. I wonder what's keeping Muffin?"

Palmer flushed at the mention of their small friend. "Maybe she's too mad at me to come see us off."

"If you're feeling guilty, don't bother," Lisa told her scornfully. "At first, Muffin was really upset, but I think she's handling the whole thing pretty well. She still wants to be Geordie's pen pal. In fact, she's already sent him another crossword puzzle."

"Good for her," Shanon exclaimed, grinning. "While we're on the subject, let's check the mail one last time before we leave."

"What for?" Amy and Lisa sighed in unison.

"Because I say so," Shanon commanded. And linking her arms through theirs, she marched them off to Booth Hall.

By the time they crossed the quad, all four girls were feeling better. And their spirits soared when they checked out the mailroom—every single one of the 3-D cubbyholes was occupied!

"I'm afraid to open mine," Lisa said, giggling nervously.

"Me, too," Amy seconded. "Why don't you read yours first, Shanon."

Dear Shanon,
In case you're wondering, the reason I haven't sent you

my one word description is that I've been trying very hard to find just the right one. But now I think I've got it: you're a custom-designed race car. That means you're stable when you hit the corners and dependable on the straightaway. Plus, you've got incredible style and grace under pressure.

It's hard to tell you how much you mean to me without getting too mushy. I hope you already know.

Have an out-of-the-world vacation!

Love,
Mars

P.S. Mr. Fixit, your favorite mechanic, revved up a few motors. They're now running on all cylinders!

"The style and grace part is so sweet," Amy sighed. "But I don't understand the P.S."

Shanon's eyes sparkled with secret amusement. "You're not supposed to. Okay, on the count of three, everybody rip open those envelopes!"

Dear Amy,

Sorry I haven't written—but I've been too embarrassed. My visit with Tricia was a total disaster. I couldn't think of a thing I wanted to say to her, and I was very relieved when the weekend was finally over. She must have felt the same way because she hasn't written since.

When we were in Figaro's, I wanted to tell you that I spent most of my time with Tricia comparing her to you. Guess what? There's no contest! You're a real person—funny, warm, and not afraid to let the world know who you are. And that's a million times better than any fantasy I've ever had.

Even though I'm the planet's biggest goofus, please keep writing to me.

Your pen pal (I hope),
John

Dear Lisa,

I'll accept your apology if you'll accept mine. You were a very good friend to want to help Muffin, even if things did go a little haywire.

After I got the Unknown Pen Pal business straight, I realized what a jerk I was to break up the great thing we've got going. Geordie really enjoyed the Muffin/Lisa letters. I want you to know it's okay with me if you still write him once in a while—as long as they're not love letters!

Now, about Bastille Day—get out your tricolor, because you and I are going to storm the barricades! Au revoir, chérie—and this time it means, "Till we meet again."

Yours,
Rob

Dear Unknown Pen Pal,

Will the real Palmer Durand please stand up? When I met her in the pizza parlor, I thought she was pretty terrific. If you ever stop playing games long enough to find her, tell her I'd like to get to know her better.

"Sincerely,"
Geordie Randolph

Lisa didn't bother to hide her grin. "I guess he told you off."

Palmer wasn't the least bit fazed. "'Now that I've got his

attention, the rest should be a snap," she said with a self-satisfied smile.

Just then Muffin dashed up to the four Foxes, her eyes wide with excitement. "I've been looking all over for you! Channel Five—talk show—Sam!" all came out in a breathless stream. "Hurry up," she cried. And without further explanation, she grabbed Palmer's hand and dragged her off toward Fox Hall's common room.

"What's that all about?" Amy queried.

Lisa shrugged. "I don't know, but I'm not going to miss it."

The group of girls already gathered around the large-screen TV set reluctantly made room for the newcomers.

"Come on, Palmer—you can't miss a minute of this," Muffin instructed, directing her to a spot on the front row.

Palmer sat down just as a husky-voiced deejay announced, "And now I'd liked to introduce the winner of the statewide contest—Brighton's own Sam O'Leary. He's usually behind the drums, but today he's doing the vocal on his song, 'Holding Hands.' "

"I can't believe it!" Shanon exclaimed, pushing closer.

"Sh-h-h-h-h!" the crowd shushed her.

As Sam walked onstage, Palmer could tell he was nervous. When he disengaged the hand microphone from its stand, his fingers were shaking. As soon as the group behind him began the intro, though, he seemed to relax.

The melody of the song was both upbeat and poignant. But it was the words that wove a magic spell over the audience. . . .

For the first time, Palmer really understood their meaning. "I wish I were there to tell him how wonderful his song is," she whispered to Amy when the verse was over and the band segued into the bridge.

Her roommate reached over to squeeze her fingers. "You can write that in your next letter."

Though Palmer nodded agreement, she watched the rest of the performance with a heavy heart. She realized how badly she had treated Sam, and she was sure he'd never want to hear from her again.

But as the last notes drifted away, the camera zoomed in for a close-up of his face. "I'd like to thank my mom and dad—and the band of course. And I'd like to say 'hi' to a special friend of mine. That was for you, Palmer. I hope you still have my address," he said, smiling.

Fadeout.

There was a moment of awed silence, then sheer bedlam broke out.

Palmer had scarcely caught her breath when she was almost buried under a pile of jubilant, squealing suitemates.

"Palmer Durand, you're the luckiest girl I've ever met!" Amy said. "How in the world do you do it?"

"Oh, it's nothing," Palmer said breezily. "I *told* you Sam thinks I've got gorgeous hands."

CHAPTER EIGHTEEN

"I don't know which is better—three days of freedom, or having all our pen pal problems solved," Lisa said as the girls from Suite 3-D stood in front of the dorm waiting for their ride into Brighton.

Amy sighed happily. "The combination is a real killer."

"It isn't too late for you to change your mind, Muffin," Shanon said. "There's always room for one more at my house."

"Next time, for sure. My parents said they might drop by for a visit this weekend." The small girl grinned mischievously, adding, "But for now, how about bringing back enough of your mom's home-baked goodies to last until the end of the term."

Shanon ruffled Muffin's hair affectionately. "You can count on it."

"Wow! Would you look at what's coming down the street!" Amy exclaimed.

Four heads immediately swiveled toward an awesome silver limousine cruising along the main avenue of the Alma campus.

Lisa let out a low whistle. "I haven't seen anything like that since the last Inaugural Parade."

"Now that's what I call a set of wheels," Palmer breathed as the impressive automobile purred to a stop in front of Fox Hall.

A uniformed chauffeur emerged. As he strode up the steps, he touched the brim of his cap, murmuring a deep, "Good afternoon, ladies."

Lisa covered her mouth to hold back a laugh. "He reminds me of a character in a movie," she said as soon as the man was out of earshot.

"Right—Frankenstein!" Amy snorted. "I bet he wears that high collar so no one will notice the bolt in his neck," she added.

All the girls began giggling at the thought, but the hilarity was abruptly cut short as the luggage-ladened man reappeared. This time, however, Lorraine Murphy was walking behind him, her eyes fixed on the chauffeur's rigid back.

The redhead was almost at the curb when she suddenly stopped and turned around to face them. "Shanon, may I speak with you in private?"

Before she could respond, Shanon's friends formed a protective circle around her.

"She doesn't want to hear anything you have to say," Lisa spoke up.

"Yes, I do." Shanon disengaged herself from the bunch with the instruction, "You guys head for the gate to meet Dad. I'll catch up with you in a few minutes."

As the others edged reluctantly away, Shanon marched down the steps to confront Lorraine. For a moment, the two girls stared at each other without speaking.

Lorraine finally broke the silence. "I don't suppose you know that I've been expelled."

Shanon swallowed hard. "I'm so sorry."

"I'm not. I've hated this stupid campus from the moment I stepped foot on it."

Beneath the bitterness that hardened the tall girl's face, Shanon detected a deep hurt and sadness. "Why did you do it, Lorraine?" she asked. "You're smart enough to get an A without cheating."

"I didn't do it for the grade. I did it to get back at you."

The unexpected revelation made Shanon gasp. "For what?"

"For having so much more than I have."

"You've got to be kidding!" Shanon exclaimed. "That silk blouse you're wearing is worth more than my entire wardrobe. And what your father spent on your luggage would pay my tuition for a whole year." But even as Shanon was protesting, she knew that wasn't the point.

"I'm not talking about money." Lorraine met her gaze defiantly. "I'm talking about love. I've never seen anything like those letters your folks sent you. I was jealous because your family cares and mine doesn't, and I wanted to punish you for it."

A huge lump rose in Shanon's throat. She knew that nothing she could say would ease the other girl's pain.

"I'm not good at apologies," Lorraine went on, "so I won't bother to say I'm sorry. I just want you to know that in spite of what I did, I like you very much, Shanon."

"We have to go now, Miss Lorraine. It wouldn't do for you to be late your first day at Hillsdale Academy," the chauffeur interrupted.

"Heaven forbid," his employer's daughter said sarcastically. "I just love new schools—I wonder how long it'll take for them to throw me out of this one?"

As Lorraine turned toward the car, Shanon touched her shoulder. "When you get settled at Hillsdale, send me your address. We can be pen pals," she said.

Some of the resentment drained from Lorraine's eyes, and a small smile flickered across her face. Blinking rapidly, she squeezed Shanon's fingers.

Shanon watched the limousine pull away from the curb, then ran to join her waiting friends. To her relief, no one asked for the details of her parting with Lorraine. One day she would tell them, but for now it was just too painful to share.

The five friends stood silent, each lost in her own thoughts. Then Palmer began to hum Sam's new song. Amy added her soft alto, extending her hand to her roommate. The gesture started a chain reaction that quickly linked all the girls in a circle. By an unspoken agreement, "Holding Hands" had become the Foxes' theme song.

"Toot—toot!" A blast from the horn of Mr. Davis's approaching station wagon ended the emotional moment.

"I forgot to mention that we'll be sort of camping out this weekend," Shanon revealed. "My room isn't large enough for all of us, so Mom is setting up four cots in the basement."

"I thought you'd had enough togetherness," Lisa teased.

Shanon giggled. "I suppose I can stand a few more days."

Before the happy quartet scrambled into the car, they surrounded Muffin, enveloping her in a group bear hug.

"I'll take good care of 3-D while you're gone," Muffin promised.

"Forget the suite," Lisa said, flashing a broad grin. "Just be sure you check the mail!"

115

CHAPTER NINETEEN

———◆———

Dear John,

I wish you could've come to the party at Shanon's house last weekend. Mr. and Mrs. Davis threw their version of my Jiating Jiè, complete with firecrackers and red-wrapped gifts for everyone.

The food was out of this world! Grandma Davis could run Julia Child into retirement. We ate so much that I was sure Mr. Davis would have to haul us back to school in a pickup truck.

But the best part of the celebration came after we finished eating. As a surprise, Shanon's mom had arranged a four-way conference call. Palmer, Lisa, and I all reached out and touched our parents at the same time. It was absolutely wild, with everyone talking at once, but I think it was the best phone call ever.

Before I say good-bye, I have to tell you that I really loved your letter. I'll probably get to know a lot of people in my life, but I don't think there will ever be anyone quite like you. I've been practicing drawing Chinese characters so that I could end with a very special message.

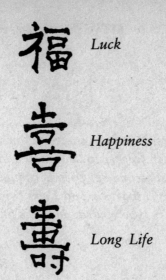

Luck

Happiness

Long Life

Amy

Dear Sam,

   I've never been hungry in my whole life. And if I want something, all I have to do is ask my parents for it. Your song made me think of other people for a change. The message came through even clearer during my visit to the Davises' house. Shanon's mom and dad volunteer some of their time at a children's shelter. Even Shanon's sister, Doreen, gets into the act. Her class at school holds car washes to raise money to feed the kids in Ethiopia.

   I think the whole experience has made me a better person. I can't promise that from now on I'll be totally sensitive and unselfish. But at least I'm going to try. If I only hit the target half the time, that will be 100 percent better than I'm doing now!

   "Holding Hands" might not make the top 40, and you

117

*may never play it on MTV. But to me, you really are a
Super-Star.*

*Love,
Palmer*

Dear Geordie,

The real *Palmer Durand is someone I'm still looking for.
I'd like very much for her to be honest and sincere. I also
want her to be someone her friends can always count on.*

*My third wish is that you and I can continue to be pen
pals. That way, maybe you can help me find her.*

*Yours truly,
Palmer*

Dear Mars,

*I think this vacation brought the Foxes a lot closer to-
gether. Every night we stayed awake very late talking about
everything we could think of. We all played the description
game, too. These are the words I chose to describe my
friends:*

Amy is a fortune cookie—*crispy-sweet and full of good
advice.*

Lisa is a scalpel—*sharp, and just right for cutting through
to heal whatever ails you.*

Palmer was the hardest, but I finally got it. She's a cactus
flower. *You have to fight your way through the thorns, but
there's true softness and beauty under the prickly exterior.*

I've saved the best for last. Mars, you're my garage, *a safe
place to park when traffic is heavy or my battery needs
recharging.*

*Till next time,
Shanon*

Dear Rob,

The weekend was superior! After we all finished talking to our families, Shanon's grandmother gave us wool mufflers she had knitted for us. Shanon's is green, Amy's is bright red, and of course Palmer's is blue—the exact color of her eyes—and mine looks like a rainbow.

I can hardly wait until Bastille Day. And I'm so glad everything is straight between us now. I was beginning to feel like Marie Antoinette on the way to the guillotine!

Now that the break is over, we're back to normal. Not "normal" boring, though—just "normal" normal. Which means that our favorite thing to do is read the mail from Ardsley.

Toodles,
Lisa

Dear Lisa,

Nothing could be "normal" or "boring" in Suite 3-D at Alma Stephens!

Check you later,
Rob

Something to write home about . . .
                        another new Pen Pals story!

PEN PALS # 12: LISA'S SECRET

What's wrong with Lisa? Not even Shanon can find out what's made Lisa change into a grouch overnight. She's irritable, moody, and snaps at everyone. She isn't even cheered up by an invitation to Maggie and Dan's wedding! When the girls hear that Lisa has stopped writing her pen pal, they *know* it's serious. They team up to solve the mystery, but then Lisa announces she's going home, leaving Suite 3-D. But she'll be back . . . right?

P.S. Have you missed any Pen Pals? Catch up now!

PEN PALS #1: BOYS WANTED!

Suitemates Lisa, Shanon, Amy, and Palmer love the Alma Stephens School for Girls. There's only one problem—no boys! So the girls put an ad in the newspaper of the nearby Ardsley Academy for Boys asking for male pen pals.

PEN PALS #2: TOO CUTE FOR WORDS

Palmer, the rich girl from Florida, has never been one for playing by the rules. So when she wants Amy's pen pal, Simmie, instead of her own, she simply takes him.

PEN PALS #3: P.S. FORGET IT!

Palmer is out to prove that her pen pal is the best—and her suitemate Lisa's is a jerk. When Lisa receives strange letters and a mysterious prank gift, it looks as if Palmer may be right. But does she have to be so smug about it?

PEN PALS #4: NO CREEPS NEED APPLY

Palmer takes up tennis so she can play in the Alma-Ardsley tennis tournament with her pen pal, Simmie Randolph III. But when Palmer finds herself playing *against*—not *with*—her super-competitive pen pal, she realizes that winning the game could mean losing *him*!

PEN PALS #5: SAM THE SHAM

Palmer has a new pen pal. His name is Sam O'Leary, and he seems absolutely perfect! Palmer is walking on air. She can't think or talk about anything but Sam—even when she's supposed to be tutoring Gabby, a third-grader from town. Palmer thinks it's a drag, until she realizes just how much she means to little Gabby. And just in time, too—she needs something to distract her from her own problems when it appears that there *is* no Sam O'Leary at Ardsley.

PEN PALS #6: AMY'S SONG

The Alma Stephens School is buzzing with excitement—the girls are going to London! Amy is most excited of all. She and her pen pal John have written a song together, and one of the Ardsley boys has arranged for her to sing it in a London club. Amy and her suitemates plot and scheme to get out from under the watchful eye of their chaperone, but it's harder than they thought it would be. It looks as if Amy will never get her big break!

PEN PALS #7: HANDLE WITH CARE

Shanon is tired of standing in Lisa's shadow. She wants to be thought of as her own person. So she decides to run for Student Council representative—against Lisa!

PEN PALS #8: SEALED WITH A KISS

When the Ardsley and Alma drama departments join forces to produce a rock musical, Lisa and Amy audition just for fun. Lisa lands a place in the chorus, but Amy gets a leading role. Lisa can't help feeling a little jealous, especially when her pen pal Rob also gets a leading role—opposite Amy.

PEN PALS #9: STOLEN PEN PALS

Shanon, Lisa, Amy, and Palmer have been very happy with their pen pals—but now they have competition! Four very preppy—and very pretty—girls from Brier Hall have advertised for Ardsley pen pals. And pen pals they get—including Rob, Mars, and John!

PEN PALS #10: PALMER AT YOUR SERVICE

Palmer's broke! Because of her low grades her parents have cut her allowance. Now she needs to find ways to make money and fast! The Foxes put their heads together to help Palmer with quick money-making schemes *and* to help her with her grades. But they can't do it all. Palmer has to help herself. But will snobby Palmer be able to handle a waitress job?